Albert's Journey into the Universe

...tim; plummer...

Copyright © 2023 ...tim; plummer...

All rights reserved. No part of this book may be reproduced, stored, or transmitted by any means—whether auditory, graphic, mechanical, or electronic—without written permission of both publisher and author, except in the case of brief excerpts used in critical articles and reviews. Unauthorized reproduction of any part of this work is illegal and is punishable by law.

ISBN: 979-8-88640-893-5 (sc)
ISBN: 979-8-88640-894-2 (hc)
ISBN: 979-8-88640-895-9 (e)

Because of the dynamic nature of the Internet, any web addresses or links contained in this book may have changed since publication and may no longer be valid. The views expressed in this work are solely those of the author and do not necessarily reflect the views of the publisher, and the publisher hereby disclaims any responsibility for them.

One Galleria Blvd., Suite 1900, Metairie, LA 70001
1-888-421-2397

CONTENTS

Chapter 1	The Challenge Arrives	1
Chapter 2	Infinity and Beyond	15
Chapter 3	Wonders Within	32
Chapter 4	The Visitors	43
Chapter 5	New Friendships	57
Chapter 6	Spreading the Wisdom	67
Chapter 7	New and Old Creations	78
Chapter 8	Preparations Begin	88
Chapter 9	Power Play	101
Chapter 10	The Tour Begins	113
Chapter 11	Group Consciousness	122
Chapter 12	Opposition Exposed	134
Chapter 13	Consciousness Density	144
Chapter 14	Dream Reality	151
Chapter 15	Leading to the Grand Finale	162
Chapter 16	Abundance of Love	171
Chapter 17	Epilog	178

INTRODUCTION

The inspiration for Albert's Journey was gradual. Like many others I feel that we can co-create a better existence. Mankind has just begun learning about or remembering our true relationship with our reality (each other and the planet). The visions I had as a child did not appear to be manifesting. When you look at mainstream programing it is clear that fear is the emotion that is stimulated for the masses.

How could this emotion of fear be used for nefarious purposes? You will find out by reading this book that I am playful in my perception of existing knowledge or mainstream propaganda. You may even want to put what is written in a category that you can dismiss. You will miss some fun in the playground of life if you do this.

The intent of this story is to inspire new possibilities so our children and grandchildren can live here and prosper in a society that supports the value that they bring by living their passions.

I have many wonderful writers that I thank for bringing information to the world that I may have worked into the story line. We all stand on the shoulders of others that contribute to the design of a better playing field.

The story takes place in the future which is the biggest reason to make it a fiction book. The potential for mankind I believe to be very real;

(just my inner knowingness). I am also a bit of a realist. The path of blind consent to a system will not evolve us. In the story a new paradigm is already in the blossoming stage so most everyone is alert to any self-serving harmful intentions. These harmful intentions are not given any real energy that they need to sustain them.

Albert has gone through the changes that brought this new awareness paradigm about. Albert's children however have been raised in this brave new world. They do not comprehend the past dogmas that ruled society. The use of fear was a primitive sociological experience that they no longer needed to experience. Albert and his adult friends reminded them to be grateful for the glorious freedom they had. The adults also nourished the young minds by allowing them to find the value they bring, encouraging them to find what make them happy then develop it.

There is no monetary system as we know it in the story. The ideas of currency are also primitive. This is a resource/value based global society where the planet Earth is treated like a living organism that takes care of its individual cells, creating a healthy environment for all inhabitants. Thus creating cooperation between man and nature that is in line with growth instead of decay.

Some of the theories that are presented in these pages are my favorites; I was not there at the creation of the universe to my currant recollection. I do not have firsthand knowledge and I am not a witness to this event. I hope you find this comment comical. I do! Let this be my disclaimer. Ha!!

When the book first started out it was written to become a graphic novel. At this point a wonderful individual came into my life journey to help with the illustrations. Albert's Journey was being shared on a web site that has members around the world. The story was released in short versions that left cliff hangers for the next episode. Corina Thornton stepped in with some of the best creations that are shared on these pages. Corina lives in Ireland so the distance factor played a role in keeping the project from blossoming early. We prevailed on many occasions and I am very grateful to know and have worked with this wonderful spirit.

The book took on a metamorphosis as things progressed. The idea of making the story into a play like format came after the book was complete as a potential comic book growing into a graphic novel. Patricia Lewis is another great spirit that helped this project along. With her editing and some added insights from gary-david; Albert's Journey took on a whole new purpose in the playground. The book is available as a story line or in play format.

A group of wonderful people got together to perform Albert's Journey in its new format. We met for an hour and a half once a week on conference calls to record each chapter. All of the characters did a marvelous job playing their parts and with efforts it will be released for public enjoyment someday coming up. In the meantime I want to put a shout out of appreciation to all who participated.

This Audio concept was designed to bring fun to the usual monotone versions of an audio book. No offence intended to the authors and or producers of some great works, we just wanted a new flare to make things with a little more excitement. This project is still in the works and has great promise.

As you read the story please look for any gems of wisdom. I make no claims to be a guru or expert on any subject but I feel that the answers are simple. I am a simple man so I just share what rings true for me. I have great fun working on Albert's Journey and my wish is that you have just as much fun reading it.

Best Regards,

Iam Steward (tim of the family plummer)

COMMENTS

Albert's Journey is a playful fantasy that will capture your heart. This story is destined to become one of the greatest favorites for dreamers of all ages. Those that are capable of imagining reality into existence will have great fun traveling with the pioneers of the universe within these pages. Open your heart and mind to new possibilities that may seem out of reach but just may be within our grasp.

Above all; have fun!!

Elaine Bennett

I had the pleasure to read Albert's Journey, if you do not understand consciousness this is a book that will allow you to learn. The most beautiful part is that it allows you to dream and think outside of the box, solving everyday major world problems. I would suggest you approach it with an open mind, happy heart and be prepared to be wowed!!!!!

MoonGoddess777
namaste'

CHAPTER 1

THE CHALLENGE ARRIVES

This story takes place as the big puzzle picture is coming together and mankind is reaching towards new visions in this Garden Universe. Like most stories we have to choose a starting point, this story has beginnings and endings throughout although the great change began one fine day with the arrival of a special package from a great team of minds.

It is the year 2045 and the world has transformed into a balance between man and nature. The genius that arose from the world's inhabitants has progressed human existence to new levels. Creations came from all cultures that enriched everyone's life. Understanding creation itself was within our reach as well as the cosmic comic realization that we know nothing in comparison to what there is to learn. People have embraced the universe where they live. The natural love for one's self has brought about a new consciousness within everyone. No longer is humanity controlled by outside authority. Men and women are all self-leaders, value producers and value creators. Humanity came around to rescue itself without relying on Governments, deities, aliens or Calvary coming to the rescue; looking within for answers.

ALBERT JENNINGS is 95 years old and looks as if he is only thirty. His six foot frame was in perfect health and his features were that of middle aged man. There was not even a speck of grey in his naturally brown hair. Only his laugh lines were pronounced on his face. He has been through the chaos that preceded the loving environment that everyone shares. That experience left him with a never ending gratefulness that humanity chose to save itself.

ALBERT's wife is Mary, they met 12 years earlier and they still could not get enough of each other. Never had Albert met such a goddess as Mary. Her natural beauty came from within as well as her well-kept physical vessel. She was also in what we now consider later years. At the age of 85 she and Albert started on having children. From the very beginning of their relationship they got along. There was never any play for the upper hand. Both Mary and Albert loved creating together and individually. They both supported and respected each other. When they met, the playground of life became so much fun and neither one of them felt it necessary to bring harm to the other. Since they were both self-leaders they mixed well together. Like dancing galaxies, they became one yet remained separate. Each one absorbed energy from the other while sharing their ideas freely with each other. The balance of energy flowed without ego.

Now Albert does what he loves best and that is to develop new technology in the space industry. Albert works <u>with</u> Universal Space Exploration or USE. Their motto is <u>use all your abilities</u>. USE also realized that everything is a part of the universe and we only have the use and not ownership. It is not necessary for everyone to "own" everything when we only use it when we need it. We create using our natural abilities along with the elements at our disposal. We must care for or steward what we use to allow the value to perpetuate.

USE has successfully taken over the lead in space exploration. Albert's work in creating an artificial gravity onboard spacecraft has allowed mankind to withstand living in space for extended periods of time. His current project is improving inertia dampeners, with the starships being built having a gravitational field built into the craft there was still challenges overcoming inertia. Spacecraft now have the capability to reach the speed of a Tachyon Particle. We called this speed warp drive but going into warp drive is still a little challenging. Albert thinks it is kind of funny that when mankind reached the speed of a tachyon they called it warp drive. It does warp the fabric of time/ space. George Hartman was the one that confirmed the existence of tachyon particle back in the year 2027.

The realization that we are all miracles of a much larger consciousness is now leading us towards becoming a cosmic civilization within the universe. The possibility for societies blossoming has always existed and it was suppressed by generations of intentional confusions perpetrated by a small percentage of the population. Men and women began awakening in the early part of the century as small groups began pulling together. In 2008, the awakening started reaching more people. Albert was a part of one of these groups that was influential in bringing about real conscious reform. Once you realize your connection with the universe, you are on a lifetime quest. Mostly though, Albert is and has always been his own self-leader. So he did not join most groups, he did however support their positive actions.

Society now is based on love and balance. A new quantum language was spoken by all. This language brought clarity that exposed intent. It was not possible any longer to contract without closure. The people that cheated their way, stifling growth, have all been exposed and the illusions of power that they created have been stripped away from them. It took individuals finding their real values as to the miracle of existence that they are the uniqueness that they bring and the vision of what is possible. The vibration of love has led us into a new paradigm for all. Most everyone was sovereign. Everyone was self-guided by the light of love within. Travel around the world was done freely as the concept of ownership was dissolved borders were also dissolved. We are all kings and queens of our kingdom within and we are using the space around us. Man decided to improve where ever they were to create the greatest, the best kingdom imaginable. The concept of borders has taken a comical spin or the realization that each individual has their own self-imposed borders and trespassing was granted through love. We are the kings and queens of the space we are in wherever we are. We only allow others to expand their kingdom into our kingdom. Royalty is within, we do not need titles. These paradigm shifts are what ushered in a new age. Mankind was now in an organic society where each cell is brought to full health to bring about a healthy planet.

One morning as Albert was pulling into work, his direct communicator went off. It was Albert's wife, MARY; she was calling to make arrangements with him for lunch.

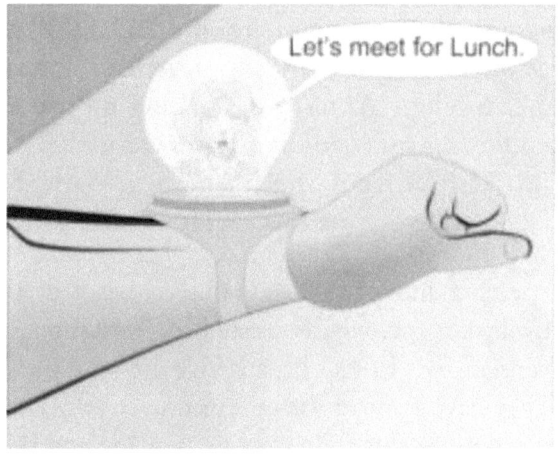

ALBERT could feel immense excitement as he approached his friend and co-worker, Bill. Albert responded to Mary briefly; "this will not be a normal day in this building. It sure is alive with excitement. I'll explain at lunch. Bye".

BILL waved Albert along saying; "come see this. Everyone is excited about the data we have received on this incoming shipment, we are into some surprises. This artifact we are receiving promises to bring new integration to the world."

As they entered the computer room, ALBERT noticed that everyone was buzzing with enthusiasm. ALBERT was directed to screen number 6 where Anna was working on the teleportation device that could transport goods all over the globe. A shipment of goods had just arrived from South America. With that shipment was a surprise item. Everyone was curious as to what it could be.

As Bill was peering into Anna's computer he noted; this shipment came from Evolution Inc. where research on evolution is done. They are saying "we sent this to you because we are stumped". What does that mean? They have some of the best minds, so why would they look to us? There is more to this than they are sharing and they must have a reason.

> As the full report downloaded, ALBERT and BILL headed down to the receiving station to get a closer look. They listened to the report on their clip on computers that could project images in front of them. ALBERT used MARY's voice on his PC's voice response as she had a melody in her voice tones.

The receiving station had such a wonderful view of the city of Utopia that ALBERT always stopped to appreciate the scenery. It is not just the view but also the energy coming from the populace. He is always amazed that as our consciousness progressed we learned how to feel the energy field around us and that we have turned it around to such a positive balance. Everyone is moving around with such purpose and intent, they are finally happy or at peace with who they are. This energy resonated; a vibration that could be felt by those that took the time out to feel it.

ALBERT and BILL were looking at the object from Evolution Inc., it appeared to be from outer space. ALBERT learned a long time ago, however, not to underestimate the genius of his fellow man, so he was full of questions.

Bill wanted to examine this with his equipment. He motioned to the receiving crew saying;" let's move this puppy to our laboratory where we can really look at this miniature quasar. There does not seem to be any power source or way to turn it on. The surface is totally smooth and reflects all light. On the lower rim here is an inscription that translates to "treasure", which was scanned with ultra violet light. Wow, even with infrared and other known spectrums of light they found nothing else. I believe it was made by man, who, when and how still remains a mystery, among many other things".

Albert also noted; in this report from Evolution Inc., "they said it had been in storage since 2010. It was a custodian's dog, who brought their attention to it. The dog entered the storage room and began to howl. This howl was not a painful howl rather it was closer to singing". "How strange"!!!!

Albert continued;" we could check it with a multi-frequency receiver too. Hmmm"!!

With a perplexed look Bill exclaimed; "maybe the reason we cannot turn it on is because it is already on".

You could see Albert's thoughtfulness as he responded; "in 2010, there was no energy source that could keep anything running this long. Remember the world was going through an energy crisis back then and we were just developing new sources and old sources were being reworked".

Chuckling, Bill replied; Yeah!! "I'm glad we woke up, eh"?

ALBERT placed the object on a pedestal. Then they continued on with the background research before starting to study the object on their own.

Later that morning, MARY arrived for ALBERT and her lunch date. ALBERT filled her in about the morning's events.

They headed towards the restaurant together passing by the Library of Science and Natural History, which was MARY's favorite hiding hole. She would spend hours there in her free time.

The display in the entrance window was a three dimensional hologram of the mythological strong man, Samson, chained to two pillars, as in the story of old. One pillar was labeled "Government" and the other pillar was labeled "Religion". Tearing down these two pillars is what really freed mankind and allowed prosperity.

Tugging Albert's arm Mary pulled him inside for a quick detour; "ALBERT, there is something I remember seeing in here that may shine a light on your new project".

"I was in here a couple weeks ago and I was looking for a book on cultural diversity, when I saw something like your object in a picture inside one of the books. At the time it looked interesting, however, I thumbed past it because it was not what I was looking for. We can check the book out and look at it tonight at home".

They found the book called <u>The Chaos and Order Ahead</u> written by Anthony Hoggins, published and copy written in November, 2009. Albert checked it out by scanning it through his PC and they went to lunch. All books and information are available in the worldwide database; however, physical books are still favored by a lot of people.

MARY and ALBERT talked more at lunch while sitting on a balcony overlooking central Utopia as transport vehicles passed overhead making their humming, bubbling sounds. There was a cool breeze and the sky was a wonderful blue color with only a few billowing clouds. It does not get any better than this, although most could find the rainbow in any type of weather. The mountains to the West were still capped in white and the tree line had different shades of green.

At the conclusion of their lunch Albert suggested; "we have met so many lifelong friends in our journey so far. We should call Myra, and get her to look at this with us. She loves this kind of research and we have not seen her in months".

Mary got excited; "I would love to see her". "She brings such laughter and fun wherever she goes. Her ability to find humor in things makes for such a great time. I smile just thinking about seeing her. She has such a great inquisitive spirit".

Chuckling to her-self; "let me call her."

Albert could see Mary light up; "I love seeing your child come out, Mary". "You go have fun"!

After lunch, ALBERT went back to work while MARY made her call. MARY got off her schedule while talking with MYRA. They laughed so hard that tears ran down their cheeks. This kind of fun was worthy of a schedule change. Usually miracles or insights develop out of this kind of playing.

At home that evening, after they had dinner and the children were off doing their homework, the doorbell rang then announced that MYRA was there. MARY welcomed MYRA with a hug then they went into the living quarters to join ALBERT. ALBERT greeted MYRA with a warm hug and a kiss on the cheek.

Jumping right into what was in the file regarding the object, they showed it to MYRA letting her know all that they have learned so far. Myra was also a child of advanced age. At the age of 70 she discovered the keys to longevity that helped reverse aging. Stem cell rejuvenation allowed the body to rebuild itself with younger healthier cells nourished by only the best foods for our bodies. Myra is now 90 years old and like Albert and Mary she was healthier than she was at thirty years old. Her passion was to learn the secrets to biological immortality. Her skin was as smooth as silk, without a wrinkle anywhere. Myra's other passion was gaining knowledge or getting closer to source is how she worded her love for learning. She listened with full loving intensity.

After a brief consideration Myra asked; "why did this get hidden away"? "I remember hearing about Anthony Hoggins and remember hearing that he disappeared in 2024 or 2025 after the collapse of the monetary system that the banking industry so carefully orchestrated".

(After a pause)

A small group of so-called elite felt that this collapse would bring the people of the world to depend on them more allowing for more control over the population. They were wrong, of course. Because of the new consciousness that was arising at that time within the new society the people looked within for solutions. This began the bankers' struggle to re-gain control of everyone as their illusions were now apparent and their greedy intent was toppled. This was predicted in the book Anthony wrote the previous year and he had to find safety so he disappeared. No one knows what happened to him".

"As I recall, his wife was doing experiments with raising the potential of the human brain, looking for a way to unleash the hidden potential within everyone. She was finding the connection that the mind, heart and spirit have with the universal energy field. Her research went missing as well". "Could this be part of their legacy"?

Albert's youngest child Charles was hiding in the doorway listening in on their discussion.

Albert urges Charles; come and join us. "This could be fun for a 5 year old".

Charles sat next to them with his eyes wide open with excitement. He loved his Aunty Myra and she saw the genius of his young mind.

With an inquisitive glance Charles asks; "Aunty Myra, I heard what you said and wonder why some people wanted to have control over others"? "This seems so wrong"!!

Myra smiled;" yes, dear one, it was wrong and it took a lot of will power to first see through the illusions, and then bring things to a place of honest love". " Some people are content to be governed by others even to this day. Most though were programmed to accept authority without self-awareness. Children back then were playing war games on their tech toys. The schools and media told them misinformation or partial truths. Violence was being programmed into them at an early age as if it was the natural way of living. Very little credit was given to the real visionaries that searched for the truth. Creating was stifled in the name of profit."

This all sounded so unfamiliar to Charles; "searching for truth must have been like looking for a gold nugget in a mountain of mud"!!!!!

They all chuckled at this because it was a good analogy of the way things were. Charles saw at an early age what most did not find out until later in life.

While looking at the picture of the project that was in the file Charles pointed out;

"It looks like it could spin like the top I play with sometimes".

"It may take the mind of a child to figure this out", Mary said. "That is brilliant, Charles!" "Have you tried spinning it Albert"?

Albert smiled; "not yet, we had not thought of that". "Would you like to be there tomorrow when we try this, Charles? After all, it was your idea, you should be there".

Myra asked; "can I be there also"?

"Yes, we can make this a family affair", Albert affirmed. "Mary, can you bring Penny and Brandon as well"?

Enthusiastically Mary exclaimed; "Are you kidding, we would not miss this event".

Later that night after Myra went home and the children were in bed, Mary edged her way into Albert welcoming arms, snuggling closer; "we have such geniuses in our home".

With that they fell asleep. This was a night full of lucid visual dreams. Not one of them had any idea of what an adventure they were about to partake upon.

CHAPTER 2

INFINITY AND BEYOND

When the next morning arrived there was sparkling excitement in the air. The children worked together to get breakfast then clean up afterwards. ALBERT and MARY did not want a robot housekeeper because it took away from the values the children were getting by doing things on their own. Even CHARLES, the four and three quarter year's old going on five, had his chores and he could not wait until it was his turn to be the cook. In the meantime, he was in charge of picking up the dishes for PENNY to organize in the dishwasher, and then he would clean the table and get ready for the day ahead.

> Albert calls out; "Charles, you will be riding with me today. Your mother will bring Brandon and Penny with her later. We will be leaving soon".
>
> Eagerly waiting Charles replies; "I will be ready, Daddy".

When ALBERT finally headed to his vehicle, CHARLES was pulling him along. "Come on, Dad"!

ALBERT smiled;
"Patience, Charles, I know you are excited".

Albert gave instruction to his anti-gravitation vehicle, programming the familiar course and destination to the USE building where he worked. The bubble car responded to all of Albert's instructions lifting off with hardly any noise. On the way to USE, Albert gave Charles some insight into the architecture of Utopia. The bubble car had a complete navigation system that drove itself. Albert takes his free time in wrought to teach Charles information about his surroundings.

"Charles, all the buildings are completely self-sustainable habitats. Some are part of the eco villages belonging to a collaborative which allows them to share data. Of course we all have access to the world data bank; however the Eco Collaborative has their focus on specialized subjects. Each structure has its own power source. In case of any hazardous outside conditions, the buildings could all maintain energy control for the inhabitants without outside help or interference." "Getting energy self-sufficient only made sense after the grid failures that followed any storms or catastrophic events".

> "Charles, all the water is recycled, treated and re-used. Rain water or snow is captured from the structures then distributed where needed. In case of just about any kind of disaster, the buildings would adapt to the surroundings or circumstances. Plexiglas shields would be raised to protect the building and those inside. This shield also served to create a greenhouse effect within the building where enough food was grown to sustain the population inside".

"These Plexiglas bubble cars allowed the commerce between the buildings". "Riding in them is fun! Isn't it, Charles"? "There are very few roads anymore so nature is no longer cluttered with concrete, asphalt, rows of advertising or hanging wires. Most of the trees you see have been to bring back the forest. They are not much older than you, Charles" "When construction started in 2019, the architect and engineers were all skilled creators. I am proud to say they are our friends. There are several utopian cities and we are lucky to live in this one because it is the safest in the world".

"The Miracle Building was the first one constructed. The design of a Taurus energy field was chosen to allow for the natural flow of energy. Then tourism funded the rest of the city. Everything is spread out with the land being cared for between structures. People from all over the world came to see what man could achieve. This was a design that not only housed people but also made them self-sufficient and safe. Natural disasters were no longer a concern. The city of the future was right here".

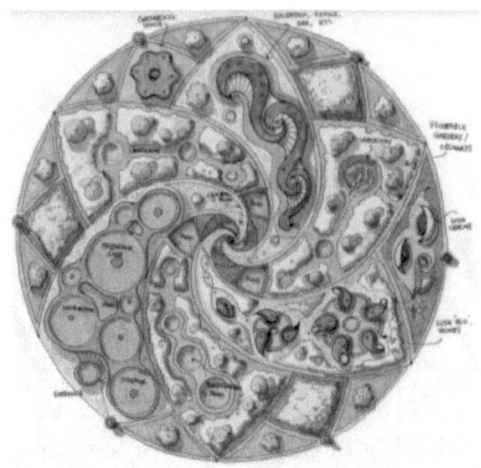

ALBERT always talked to CHARLES like this. It amazed ALBERT at how much CHARLES absorbed. ALBERT felt it was important that his children knew how this infrastructure worked. Children would understand and integrate better than most adults at times, as children are full of miracles.

ALBERT and CHARLES arrived at USE then hurried to the lab. BILL was already there and could not wait to talk to ALBERT about what he had discovered.

Bill met Albert and Charles at the door saying; "when I arrived here this morning the lights were off and there were small beams of light shining in every direction from the object. No one ever noticed this before because it was kept in a crate all this time".

As BILL went to shut off the lights ALBERT stopped him; "let's wait a few more minutes before you shut off the lights. Mary is bringing Brandon and Penny. Myra is also on her way. They will all be here soon".

"Cool", Bill replied; "I would love to see them. We are all in for a treat". "We should move to the auditorium where we have plenty of open space".

After everyone had arrived, ALBERT directed them into the auditorium where the object had been relocated. Once they were settled,

"Bill, Charles had a great idea as simple as spinning the object", Albert stated.

Bill placed the object on a pedestal; "great, let's start this; we will try that first"!

The gold and silver object was placed on a pedestal in the middle of the room. As BILL shut down the lights, ALBERT started spinning the object in a clockwise direction. To all of their amazement, it started spinning on its own. A peaceful sound started emitting from the object as the room filled with a holographic display of a DNA vortex. Along the ribbons and bars of the DNA strand, everyone could see the universe forming. Miniature galaxies, nebulas and solar systems filled the strand in all directions. The accuracy of the display was incredible. Then the vortex inverted in a mirror image of the first section of the strand. This continued in a circle until it met back with the source being the Gateway. At each vortex, there was a dark hole that was sucking in so much light that it glowed as bright as a star.

The multi-universe formed in front of their eyes and it all made sense. Everything is all connected as a DNA stem cell for something much greater than our wildest imagination. As the display grew in size the galaxies became clearer and soon they could see solar systems with planets and stars. Everything followed the path of the DNA strand. Each universe/duplicate universe took the shape of quasars, first expanding the universe, then contracting the universe before entering a new singularity where it all started over on its path back to the source. Each universe went into a different spectrum of light that changed the consciousness within that manifestation, like bathing in awareness. One tiny,

tiny particle of this strand was the Milky Way Galaxy. Even smaller particle was the Solar system with the planet Earth. Yet even smaller was the life on planet Earth, including each individual. Yet, each viewing person's thoughts affected the whole consciousness. Wow!

This existence was mirrored throughout the strand so everything exists at the same time. Time itself had taken on a new meaning.

ALBERT watched as CHARLES reached out for the galaxies around him. MARY started dancing with the vibration accompanying this wonderful display. ALBERT felt like he was a part of what he was experiencing. His life from birth to that day and beyond was in his mind as if it was all happening in the present moment. The progression of life became crystal clear to him, starting with the single cell organism. This was all taking place in his mind and he felt like he was a part of this creation. He realized that the universe was just a blink in eternity.

Never had any of them experienced such unity with the creator. They were taping into their right brains forming visions. The left brain was having a hard time placing what they were experiencing into context with what they believed. Energy passed through them. Around them and collided into them like the formation of a planet. Planet formations evolved around spinning mini stars that created a magnetic vortex that looped back to itself within a magnetic field. Cosmic debris would accumulate around the magnetic shield and a skin would form around the spinning mini star; creating planets. Planets were attracted to the magnetic pull of central suns, forming solar systems. Most all planets showed signs of life on the interior of the planet and only a few in comparison sustained life on both the interior and exterior. Earth was one of these special planets.

As ALBERT looked around at his family and friends he could see the energy coming from their auras, interacting with the energy of this miniature universe. He watched as their spiraling energy fields interacted with the energy in the room and with each other. New creations were formed as everything touched everything else and he realized that this went on all the time and we could not see it. As the energy collided with other energy something new was created and nothing would ever be the same. Creation is a never ending, continual process.

Just then, GEORGE, one of the building maintenance staff, walked into the room. All he saw was a spinning artifact with a humming sound and a great light show. He did not see what the others were seeing and thought they were crazy. He stopped the object from spinning, turned on the lights.

"What was wrong with everyone", George asked?

They all answered at once; "Didn't you see it Georges"? "The universe was unfolding and we were connected".

George just rolled his eyes and snickered; "What did you people take to make these hallucinations occur for you"?

"We did not do or take anything" Mary shared. "Your mind must not be allowing you to have this experience".

Myra escorted George out of the auditorium saying; "this must tap into our connection with the universe through the heart center along with the right hemisphere of our brains. Only those with a completely open mind can experience it". "Sorry George"!! "Clear up your pineal gland and connect with your heart center, then come back, my friend".

Albert stepped forward; "the answers we got here today only raise a million more questions. We will have to get experts from every field to experience this then help with those answers".

They all hugged each other and it was not like any other hug that they had shared. The energy between them all made them realize just how powerful physical contact with one another is. It is a give and take situation, leading to a new creation, a cosmic connection. They would never look at life the same way as before and this brought comfort to them all.

Albert was thinking to himself; "*We should all sit down now and discuss what they had experienced*".

Mary responded as if he spoke out loud; "Yes dear, we should discuss this".

Albert was stunned looked at MARY thinking; "*She was always aware what he was thinking and only this time was different*".

"Yes, it is different this time, Albert", Mary said. "I am actually hearing your thoughts and everyone else's thoughts in this room. It is all good positive energy".

The GROUP sat down at the table and one by one they gave an account of what they had experienced. All of them saw

and heard the universe unfold for them; however, there were subtle differences with each version.

Myra started; "I could feel all the suffering going on, all the ill-ness or dis-ease then only my levity and love allowed me to feel a powerful quenching empathy that soothed me. I felt myself reaching out and making things better. So much of the suffering was unnecessary. Self-inflicted stress related problems were easily cured".

Bill spoke next; "I felt as light as air and moved around the room observing everything in detail. I looked at things from all different perspectives, floating around freely. I traveled to various galaxies and felt that I was there for a long time".

Penny was still in a euphoric state; "I feel like I have a new voice". "How does it sound to you"? "I could feel sound take form and I could visualize all the possibilities of this fantastic playground in which we are a part. I felt like a receiver of all the vibrations that existed. I am seeing too much to explain".

Mary started helping Penny relate her experiences; "I can hear what you're thinking Penny as you struggle to put it all into words. I can help translate into words what Penny is revisiting in her mind".

Mary continued; "I feel a part of every living being everywhere with extra closeness to the ones I love and are here with me. It is like one mind amongst all of us. It is like one energy ball, that I can distinguish the individuality of us all at the same time. I have never felt such closeness to Albert, you children and our friends".

Brandon was attempting to act cool as he was not sure just what he had experienced. Haltingly; "I was close to a nebula and watched as new stars were being born. I saw a sun go nova and felt its force as it took everything in its path with it, including the consciousness of everything that had evolved in that area of the galaxy. I saw that consciousness was spread throughout the universe and how that conscious wave continued until it was received by other life forms on its path. Some of the consciousness became part of the new stars forming in the nebula".

Charles was waiting patiently for his turn, which seemed a little out of the ordinary for him. He usually wants to be first.

Albert saw Charles's excitement; "Charles, do you want to be next"?

"Yes, daddy, it was so much fun", Charles exclaimed!! "When I reached out to touch that galaxy I could feel it talking to me. Kind of like how you talk to me, daddy, only it was all at once. The room filled with a web of different colors and I could see how everything was connected. My laughter made the web shimmer, as if I was controlling it to some extent. I can still see the web only it looks different up close. I guess it is because we are all back here and close to each other. It looks so cool!!"

Albert gave the best rendition of his experience as he could. He concluded by asking; "what does this entire experience mean"? "It seems, even with cosmic awareness, we still have questions". "We still know nothing". "We plucked the grapes of the universe and still need answers".

ALBERT and BILL went back to works as MARY and the children went home. MYRA had also left for an important meeting with the scientist for biological immortality.

ALBERT's mind was sharper than it had even been. Certain truths were coming to him as if to remind him of how to keep his humanity.

Albert started talking out loud to himself; "here and now are the only things that matter. I define now why our existence in what we believed was based on our experiences. The right side of our minds lets us know that there is so much more to learn and to know. We experience the smallest fraction of what really is available. We proclaim knowledge superior to all living things, yet we are related to it all without seeing it. The cycle of time reveals the laws of cause and effect".

"For ages mankind has repeated its destructive cycle. We kept repeating mistakes that did not serve the world's inhabitants yet it served the few in power. When the populace realized that what we have been doing for centuries does not work, the people developed new ideas, and then positive change came about for everyone".

> **Albert's left brain was very busy processing his experience. It was like he could step into any place in the time stream and yet he was here and now. How does the mind comprehend? Just how far would this lead? What answers lay ahead?**
>
> **His inertia balancers came to him easily. How simple it was, once he saw it in place, complete in his mind, while experiencing it in the future. All he had to do at that point was take the process backward in his mind to where he was, and then continue forwards again. Once he explained it to Bill, who was able to bring it into a new perspective, it was a done deal. They accomplished in one afternoon what they had been researching for months.**
>
> **Albert was always able to see his projects completed and then plan for their creation. His visions now are so clear and the details are so vivid. Could all his questions get answered or would they just lead to more questions? This is what MYRA calls cosmic levity. It is kind of funny.**

Bill caught ALBERT before he left for lunch; "**ALBERT**, I have broken the inertia balancers down to its basic sub-atomic particles. I'm already working on production design and flow charts". "I'm not sure how I was able to do it so quickly"?

"Everything just flowed. I was able to spot the problems and the solution came to me in the next instant".

"We have experienced something that may affect us in ways we can only imagine", Albert answered. "We better prepare ourselves".

Albert was glad for the self-navigation in his vehicle that afternoon as he traveled home. Everything he looked at he saw through the progression of time. He looked at a tree and saw the seed, then watched it pop out of the ground. He watched it take root, then reach for the sky, form a trunk with branches and leaves. He felt the changing of the seasons, the shedding of the leaves and the rejuvenation that spring brought. All of this took place in an instant, because in the next instant he was processing something new.

Albert looked at the mountains and saw the shifting of the tectonic plates. He saw the coming and going of an ice age leaving behind great boulders from other areas of the world. He saw the erosion caused by the melting of the snow, whittling the mountain away as another mountain range got even bigger by the pressure of the tectonic plates. How can all of this be put into words?

Yet, Albert never felt more happiness. This would be overwhelming for most. He was euphoric with his new heightened awareness. Could he capture any moment in time and live it as an observer? Somehow he felt that there were no limits to what he could witness.

Albert was thinking out loud; "I remember 2008 where life was at a pivotal point with me and all humanity. Does this time hold answers to my questions about the object? I remember what I was doing that year and the strength of character I needed to just get by and start to prosper".

Albert's thoughts rambled on; Boy, that was a time of uncertainty for most people because of the rising cost of energy and goods. The scarcity of work was making many men and woman's lives decline to a point of losing all they had achieved. I can still feel all over again the desire for change and the passion to bring about a better existence for everyone, especially for the children, who deserved better, as they were not the creators of all this unnecessary strife.

Abundance was available at this time; however, it was being horded by the selfish few that thought only of power and control. These selfish individuals did not think that the majority of the people had the potential to lead themselves, so it was up to these minorities to bring order to the world in the vision that they had for their own gain. I recall all the forces used to keep the populace scrambling for survival and wallowing in ignorance.

All information was filtered through these controlling few who spun the truth to suit their agenda. They treated the world like one big mushroom farm, feeding them with dung and keeping them in the dark. Schools taught what to think and not how to think for you". No more. This new generation is already performing miracles we only dreamt of.

It was such a relief, as the few rallied for more control, to see the people rise up and turn things around. Eyes were opening for the first time as more and more men and women saw through the illusions being created. After determining the potential results, the self-leaders would not let the few in the cabal have their agenda come to pass.

How did we miss it? The answer was so simple to the loving geniuses in this time period and the task ahead was clear. Great literature was written by many who brought back into view the self-worth to the masses. This woke up the visionaries and the doers to make the changes needed. Mankind's full potential would not be recognized if it stayed on the path that they were being corralled by the controlling minority.

Albert remembered his own struggle to find the truth in a society of half-truths. His hunter instincts lead him to stalk society with the purest intent. Finding all the common denominators held by all people led me to the answers. Learning the laws of the universe led to effective change. By shedding his pre-existing paradigm of his limited belief system, he was able to move forward.

"I no longer live anyone else's paradigm", he thought; "unless it will serve the greater good for all of mankind. The universal paradigm of truth and principles is my path of discovery. Love is my guiding light".

"There must be purpose for this recapitulation I'm going through as somehow I was not tying it all in with the silver object".

"This answer must come later".

These musings all took place in a blink of an eye and Albert found that he had arrived home.

Mary met Albert as he arrived; "Albert, you will not believe what has happened to us this afternoon".

Reading ALBERT's mind; "you are so right"!!! "At this point nothing can surprise us"!

After a loving hug, they headed into their home. Mary commented that she was able to block others thoughts now; "all I have to do is watch my breathing and focus on the children or a project. This centers my mind, balancing with my left brain. I can now turn this ability on and off like a light switch. I can help you and the children to do the same".

"I have to regain control because the children had been doing things that would be considered miracles".

Charles grabbed ALBERT by the finger saying; "Daddy, watch what I can do".

When the **FAMILY** got to the pool, **CHARLES** was as excited he ran out into the middle of the pool on top of the water. He stood in the middle of the pool saying; "see, Daddy, what I can do. I just make the water hard beneath my feet".

"You make it sound so easy Charles", Albert said in amazement.

Charles playfully answered; "well it is easy! Watch this",

> **CHARLES reached for the ball that was across the pool deck. The ball started flying towards Charles' open arms only it bumped his head instead. Charles started laughing so hard that he dropped into the water. Then CHARLES came up sputtering.**

"Now I just need to learn how to catch".

Everyone's laughter was like a breath of fresh air, a brief reprieve from all the new changes. CHARLES rose out of the water and walked to the edge.

Penny wrapped a towel around Charles; "let's dry you off. Oh, you already are".

> **It was her thoughtfulness that made the gesture so meaningful.**

Albert sat down with his family; "tell me what has been going on around here today after you left for home"? "I've gotten some vivid flashback of the day's events when I walked in the door only I want to hear your stories anyway".

Brandon started rambling an Angorian Dialect.

"Stop", Mary interrupted; "**BRANDON**, dear, you're talking in the Angorian dialect. Your clicking and snapping does not make much sense to the others".

Brandon changed his speaking; "sorry about that, I know so many ways of communicating now from dialects to vibrations".

BRANDON began talking in all these different languages, speaking wisdom long forgotten and new revelations yet to be discovered.

Penny interrupted Brandon; "it is my turn now"! "I went into my room when we got home and I was still so full of happiness. I was chewing bubble gum, humming and singing when I noticed some birds stopping at my window. When I looked out the window I saw other animals approaching to listen to my melody. It reminded me of a storybook fairy tale and when I blew a bubble with my chewing gum it came out in the shape of a fairy that animated itself, flying around my room. It was so beautiful! The sounds that I make can form hard sound shapes that, if covered in an outside layer, they can be seen. I started blowing soap bubbles into shapes after that only they popped when they landed".

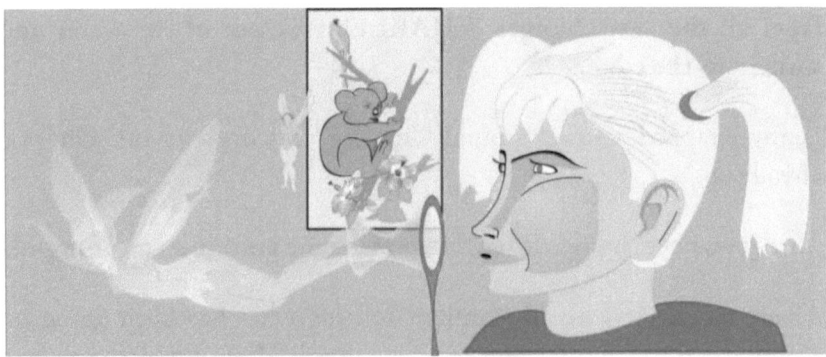

After Penny gave a little demonstration that amazed everyone they all set about doing their chores for the evening. Even the chores took on a new excitement and fun. Nothing compares to the changes still ahead.

CHAPTER 3

WONDERS WITHIN

Supper time at ALBERT and MARY's home had taken on some astounding changes. As always Brandon did the cooking only now he had access to the best recipes in the universe. He made a salmon dinner that was out of this world.

Proud of his cooking Brandon announced; "if I could have added some Volutian grubs, it would have been better". "That, plus the herbs from the dragon field of nourishments on the planet Kronis, makes a flavor that is fit for gods and goddesses".

Charles levitated the dishes bragging; "this is so cool clearing the table without leaving my seat. Look, PENNY, I can put everything on the counter for you to wash. I won't break anymore dishes".

While humming quietly washing dishes Penny's imagination went wild; "Pretty bird you dance to this melody so well. Ah, you dish soap bubbles are taking on the shape of flower that I see in the fields on rolling hills".

Mary admired her children's work; "you kids are having so much fun". "Who was it that said chores are drudgery"? "**ALBERT**, what is this world going to be like as more and more people are able to touch into their inner potential? I can't wait".

Contemplating the thought; "that is a great question as I had a flash into the future where I saw creations never before imagined and an exhilarating sense of unity as if the world was functioning as one organism". "Space exploration is being accomplished in many new ways leaving the traditional spaceship mode behind. Since space crafts were at a peak in development". "Now we will use our corporal forms to travel to distant destinations. I can see the whole world celebrating the 4th of July as the great awakening day offering inner independence for all".

"With my heightened abilities I am closer to you than ever", Mary explained; "ALBERT, you are the only one that I can share visions with". "When I am close to other people, I hear the chatter in everyone's mind created by their left brain. With you, I can go much deeper".

Conspiratorially in a whisper; "that is much better than foreplay". Albert grabbed Mary's hand; "let's check that idea out, my angel".

> **ALBERT and MARY worked their way to the privacy of their room, playing and dancing mentally as they went. Once the door was closed, they embraced like a collision of cosmic forces. Never had they experienced a merging of such oneness, like two atoms merging into one. The energy field around them swirled as they joined. The energy between them could power a city, if captured and harnessed. They lay in each other arms after what seemed like an eternity of bliss then fell soundly asleep.**
>
> **The next morning, upon awakening.**

Snuggling closer, Mary capitulated; "ALBERT, my dreams were so vivid, could you see in color also? I felt like I was part of another physical universe and anything was possible in that realm".

"I had complete control in my dreams", Albert responded. "Did you"? "I traveled to different dimensions and manifested whatever I wanted. I feel so rejuvenated in ways that leaves me full of energy. In my dreams I never felt separated from you".

With tangible shivers still being shared Mary whispers; "last night was true bliss. We are going to have to do that more often"!

Albert was grinning at the thought; "you bet! I will do my part in making that happen".

"Wow, even going to work will feel different; I can hardly control my vision journeys. Thank goodness, **MARY** you are helping me so much to get that under control".

Later that morning at the USE Center, Albert arrives in Bill's lab.

"**BILL**, where are you"? "We have so much to talk about after last night". "Hmmm, where can he be"?

Clicking on his computer and speaking out loud; "I've gotten so many e-mails and these calls…. Everyone is interested in what happened yesterday. I've got to get a detailed update to the world web right now".

Adrian Adams (CEO of USE) voice was crackling over the intercom speaker; "**ALBERT**, I'd like to see you in my office at 9:30 am, please".

"No problem", Albert replied; "I'd better get a move on though, I have only 15 minutes to get all this done and get down to your office. Have you seen or heard from Bill"?

With concern, Adrian answered; "Bill has not called or checked in yet. You can fill him in later".

Later in Adrian's Office overlooking Utopia City.

After a welcoming hug, Adrian ask; "how are you, **ALBERT**"? "How are **MARY** and the children"? "So much is happening! I can hardly keep up with all the inquiries. What else is going on"?

Assuring Adrian that plans are in the works, Albert answered; "starting off, I am sure you have been briefed about yesterday's experiment".

Adrian confirmed; "Yes, I listened to your web blast and we wanted to know how you are planning to share this value with the world, like in your vision? Millions of calls are coming in and we are just encouraging patience. We are letting everyone know that we are still doing research".

"Caution is needed", Albert concerns were voiced; "we need to hold off a bit, however, go ahead get your best minds on spreading the word. This is meant to be shared with all mankind. This will be better than sliced bread, anytime".

Smiling at ALBERT's remark; "you love using those old expressions, I feel good hearing them again". "You and **BILL** are the best team we have for this job. Is one week enough time for you to be ready for the announcement to the world?"

"That will give us all the time we need", Albert assured. "We need make it clear that this will not affect everyone. As we know here at USE, this is like a gateway to your individual connection with the universe and some people are just not ready to enter through that gate".

"I believe that the individual can develop that connection within themselves, when they choose to do so. Spiritual preparation is needed and is being encouraged. Anyone that has accepted their source within or has felt their connection to the universe should not have any problems".

"**ALBERT**, make sure we know the names of everyone that helped bring this to the world, so they can share in the rewards they brought to society". "I like what you called it, 'The Gateway,' that is how it will be introduced to the world. Above all, make sure it is harmless".

Reassuring Adrian; "I believe that all it really does is stimulate or heighten all of your natural senses like a meditation tape might do. This will help everyone realize more of their potential. It is like a library in certain ways. It seems to take you where your mind naturally goes, then enhances that within you. Everyone's experience will be different, even if they are sharing the same visuals".

"Our aim is for this sharing to take place in one week, it is the Fourth of July and we could make this a true Independence Day for humanity. Is this probable Albert?"

"Yes Adrian, we will make it happen"! "You are so right about Independence Day. This fell into my vision journey from last night. Interesting"!

After the meeting, back in the lab with Albert's wrist phone ringing. Myra is calling with an update.

Myra breathlessly;" I have been so very busy since yesterday's experiment". "After I left USE, I went by the Utopian Mall and the people there just flocked to me. I was able to see right into their souls, see their auras and spot any troubles or blockages. Just by helping them clear these blockages I was able to help them feel better than they have felt for years. I showed them the power they had within themselves. It took a lot of my energy and I slept for ten hours last night. How did they know that I could help them?"

With loving assurance, Albert replies; "Myra, they felt your presence stronger than ever before. It seems our experience with what we are now calling it 'the Gateway' which enhances what we do naturally and with you it is healing. You always have had certain magnetism with people. You were the first one that you healed and they could feel your energy".

Excited Myra continued; "it is not just people that I see their ailments or suffering. I can see what is wrong with animals and plants also. I have this orchid at home that I have struggled to keep alive. When I got home last night, I saw immediately what it needed, as soon as I touched it, while moving it closer to my waterfall, it perked up. This morning it had a new bud on it. I am going to love this new ability! I can look at soil and see what it needs and I can spot un-ease in the universe immediately, and then heal it".

"In my dream state, I was able to visit all of my departed love ones. They had all ascended to a different plain of existence. At first, I entered a vertical rift in the fabric of space/time with a bright light coming from it".

"I was greeted with just a voice in my mind saying", *'Welcome Dear One, we get very few visitors from your physical three dimensional worlds with your awareness. Come we will guide you to insure your safe return.'*

"I only felt complete love! So I accepted the welcome from the spirit guide. I realized that I was also on a much higher level of existence and could feel the oneness of the cosmic consciousness of which they were a part and yet you could distinguish the individuals as well. This was pure existence without unnecessary descriptions or limits, like being a part of the energy web field that connects all matter. Looking around, I saw a matrix of beauty beyond my wildest imagination. I was returned the same way I entered, gathering intense strength that would allow me to face and heal more of our troubling world. When I awoke this morning I was filled with vigor and enthusiasm". "I'M READY TO GO".

"Everyone involved in yesterday's event have seen dramatic changes within themselves", Albert explained. "I am glad you were able to understand what you were experiencing. **MARY** has been very helpful with centering the rest of us. You may want to visit with her".

Myra replied; "I am going to see **MARY** at three o'clock at the library".

In a concerned tone Albert asks; "have you heard from **BILL**"? "He has not shown up yet and he is usually the first one here. I may have to allow one of my vision flashes to locate him".

"You know Bill", Myra said jokingly; "**he** is probable checking out every corner of the universe from every angle and perspective he can. That may take him a while".

"You are so right, **MYRA,** that fits **BILL**'s passion so perfectly. I am sure he will show up. I will call you or Mary when he does, so you know he is all right".

> **After loving farewells, MYRA and ALBERT disconnected their phone link. ALBERT started pondering things from the first arrival of the Gateway. He was intrigued by the fact that everyone felt the importance of the object before they found out what it was all about. The fact that it came from Evolution Inc. was enough to arouse excitement. Evolution Inc. is the leader in the field of conscious evolution helping millions reach new levels of enlightenment.**
>
> **There are so many great minds at Evolution Inc. and they should have been able to figure this out.**

Speaking aloud; "it took the mind of a child to unlock its secrets and enable the Gateway to operate to greater efficiency. That the Gateway seems to be always powered up only it takes spinning for it to release the full effect buried in its canister".

"This report shows holes in it. Evolution Inc. knew more than they included in this report. They did a lot of experiments with cloning and consciousness transference. Let's see, the top researcher in this field is my old friend, **PEGGY WORTHRIGHT**! I'll give her a call right now on the virtual web".

ALBERT waited for PEGGY WORTHRIGHT to answer the virtual web.

"**PEGGY**, it's great to see you again". "What can you tell me about what we are calling 'the Gateway' that was not in your report? We have had some major breakthroughs. As a matter of fact, I see a big change in you also. You look radiant".

"Thank you Albert"! "I looked at what you are calling 'the Gateway' for about a month before sending it to you. In that time I had a lot of exposure to it. It was awesome in that each day that I made contact with the Gateway, it made me feel a closer connection with the universe. My awareness increased. I thought it was the new diet I have been using. The symbol meaning 'treasure' was noticed by our team which only raised our curiosity. We did not know that the key to the treasure was locked inside our minds. I must say that your son, **CHARLES**, is a genius, just like his father".

"Thank you, **PEGGY**; that is so kind". "**CHARLES** has the advantage of having the clear mind of a child without the developed beliefs that held us back in that past age. This new generation of children that will experience the Gateway, without their belief limitations, will be light years ahead of us".

After a brief moment of pondering Peggy says; "the only thing that I can think of that was not included in the report is that, while the Gateway was in storage, we came across this mouse that we could not catch. We found small paintings on the walls by his escape hole that looked like the hieroglyphics in a pyramid. It makes more sense now that we know that the Gateway helps in the progression of conscious evolution. The mouse pictures told a story that showed the Gateway and other pictures of us chasing him. Apparently the mouse thought of us as gods that were punishing them for stealing food".

"That is very interesting, **PEGGY**. It makes sense that it would affect animals also. Have you seen this mouse again"?

"No, it seemed to have disappeared when we shipped the Gateway".

"Wow! This has taken a turn that we did not expect. This could get interesting".

Right after disconnecting his call with Peggy, Albert received another call regarding Bill.

"This is the operator at the Utopian Memorial Health Care Center. Do you have a friend named **BILL**? He is here under observation. Can you come by and see him?"

"Yes, Ma'am. I'll be right over".

Albert immediately called Mary; "**MARY**, they found **BILL**. He had not come in to work today. I just got a call from the Utopian Memorial Health Care Center saying he is there for observation. Can you join me as you may be able to help him more than the doctors can?"

Mary met Albert at the Utopian Memorial Health Care Center, speaking to the Emergency Room doctor.

"Your friend, **BILL**, appears to be outside his physical vessel and is in a waking dream state", the doctor reported. "His consciousness is gone out of his corporal body. What is going on here?"

"Well you see, **DOCTOR**, there was an experience that BILL and a few others had with the Gateway and the affects it is having on all who participated. **BILL** has a passion for looking at everything from every possible perspective. My wife, **MARY**, may be able to help him back".

Mary filled the doctor in; "I have only been able to hear the chatter of the left brain in most people, while with my husband, **ALBERT,** we meld our energies completely. If I concentrate, I should be able to help **BILL**".

EMERGENCY ROOM WHERE BILL LIES MOTIONLESS

Mary noted right away; "there is no left brain activity. It is silent and not active at all. I'll check it out, please be quite everyone".

In her mind's eye MARY sees a vision of a rift in space with a tether line leading into the rift. Mary has now been following

the tether for some time noticing that it made loops around everything she came across. It looks as if Bill had spent time checking everything out as he went further into space. After what seemed like an eternity, MARY saw BILL at the edge of a black hole in the center of a remote galaxy. BILL looked like he was dancing, as he moved around the black hole, like he was in orbit.

"**BILL**, you need to return with me". "You may get lost to us forever if you continue on your journey. Let's go back so you can tell us about all that you have discovered".

Sounding far away, Bill answers; "I am so close to being able to enter this black hole. This may be my only chance to see where all matter goes when it enters the black hole. It is my theory that the black hole vortex is our quickest way back to our heart center and back to the physical realm".

Softly pleading; "you do not know that for certain and it is risky". "**BILL**, you may not be able to return if you go in there. Your tether may break and then there is no return. You have so much more to learn before that happens".

> BILL reluctantly takes MARY's hand and they head back. As the two traveled homeward, BILL would stop every chance he had to cosmically photograph as much as he could. MARY had to keep Bill focused on the homeward bound path. When they reached the entrance to the portal, BILL took one last look around before leaving that rift in space/ time.

> Both Bill and Mary opened their eyes at the same time. Mary felt they were gone a long time while Albert reassured her that she was only gone for a few moments.

Calmly Albert speaks; "it is good to have you back with us, **BILL**". "We thought you may not want to return. **MYRA** and I felt that this would occur only we did not think of the danger you might find yourself in out there in space".

"I was not in any danger by my standards", Bill reassured. "I realized that I needed to return with **MARY** though, to share what I had learned. I am going to rest for a little while so I will meet you back at the lab later today or in the morning".

"You take all the time you need, **BILL**".

OUTSIDE THE HOSPITAL, MARY KISSED ALBERT GOOD-BYE

"I'm on my way to meet Myra at the library", Mary announced.

Playing discretionally with a purring voice into ALBERT'S MIND; "remember last night, Albert".

Albert went back to the lab to finish off his day feeling relieved and excited. He finished up his reports to the world web letting everyone know the incident with Bill. He added that he did not think there was any real danger but everyone should be aware of personal response-ability for all of our choices. Bill saw no danger, so for him there was none, that is how Bill responded.

CHAPTER 4

THE VISITORS

Albert arrives back at his lab. His desk is a mess.

"What happened in here? It looks like a bomb exploded. I should have locked up before I left".

> **ALBERT should have looked at the smudges a lot closer before he wiped them up from his desk. He would have seen that they were not arbitrary marks, they were a picture message. From behind a box in the corner of the room came a little squeak that Albert did not even hear. A small disappointed critter scampered off into the woodwork.**
>
> **Retreating into the crate that was nearby; the critter seemed to be mumbling. He raised his little arms then shrugged his shoulders, shaking his head with a series of quiet squeaks.**

Albert heard some noise; "what was that"? "Oh, it was nothing, just my imagination". Let me get into this Anthony Hoggins' book, he thought to himself. Anthony is relating his perspective on what is going on in his time. I guess this was a big part of the great paradigm shift that took place in 2010 through 2014.

This book by Anthony Hoggins, The Chaos and Order Ahead, is very interesting. It told about the secret ruling class that lasted for centuries, continually seeking control of the people. They ruled over governments, businesses, military and religions. The 3 ruling cities run by 300 families. Hoggins pointed out the need for everyone to rely on the power of self-determination while exposing the illusion of corporal outside authority. All of the right answers are within us all. All that is needed is for us to stop giving our energy or consent to what is harming others. He wrote about the miracles that we are and the miracles of which we are a part. Seek truth and remember that what we have to learn as a species is much greater than what we know. Seek wisdom and knowledge in everything, for man is capable of much more that we allow ourselves to believe. We have to get to where we know the true everlasting principles or ethics of peaceful coexistence. That is just common sense to the truth seekers and light workers. The switch from thinking with your mind to thinking with your heart is the salvation of humanity.

Becoming a sovereign individual was the driving theme within the book. Self-governing is a state of mind that is reached by developing self-responsibility or your ability to respond. We respond to everything that we contact, our emotions react to our circumstances or our environment. We, as individuals, can gain control and choose our responses towards positive outcomes with love. Never forget the true order within natural law that puts the prime creator (what others call god, the universe, the Omni universe and everything in it) first, mankind second and creations of man, such as governments, religions, businesses, monetary systems and so on under man to serve man. Hoggins further explained how the ones seeking greater control reversed this process and the masses of individuals are at the bottom being ruled by fictitious, controlling entities.

ALBERT pondered; these were all good thoughts. That it was really true for that period of time in history.

In Chapter 9 of his book, Anthony Hoggins wrote about an ancient civilization, which he had proof existence. This is where he refers to the now named Gateway and shows a picture of it. This civilization was over ten thousand years old, yet they had reached a level about which we have only dreamed. Just the child's unfettered dream of harmony would match the wonder that this ancient civilization achieved.

The description of the civilization led Albert into one of his vision journey's.

"Where Am I"? Is this a cosmic paradise, he pondered? Am I on another vision journey back to that time and place in Hoggins' book? This world is still primitive and savage as the Earth was violent in nature and in beast. How could such an advanced civilization have existed this far back in time? This is a wonder.

> **Albert chooses to go along with this journey and bring his left brain with him.**

If I can just keep my rational left brain quiet from all the chatter I can experience this vision in a different way. The chatter will stop once I got myself into contemplation and centering.

> **ALBERT entered the city he would come to know as Lemuria. This was the cradle of consciousness on our planet, the birth of the spread of knowledge for man.**

Were these ancient ancestors or co-creators of the prime creator or both?

> **Upon entering the city, ALBERT felt an energy that he had never felt before and yet it seemed so familiar. He noticed that he could feel such purpose and contentment within everyone he observed. The people were operating on a higher plain of reality as if this was heaven on Earth. Walking through the city he noticed a lot of things that reminded him of Utopia. He had a good eye for details along with a unique understanding of what it took to build such a place. He observed as people that looked so different from each other, worked together. The development of negative self-centered emotions was not a part of this life. Just the observance of the absence of greed, ego, fear, malice, coveting, usury, coercion, fraud and gossip made this a Heaven! Mankind's gene pool was not as small as it is in times to Come, so the variety of people was much greater. Here they were all working together to bring about a better existence for each other, as well as, themselves.**

It was like a bee hive of efficiency, ALBERT's rational left brain chattered on in an attempt to bring everything into a perspective he could grasp. He walked through Lemuria without being noticed by anyone.

Albert gets startled by hearing a voice; welcome old friend! I am glad you are here. Come and spend some time with me.

Albert looked around; what! "Who is it"?

The next thing Albert realizes, he is back at his desk in the lab.

His vision was so vivid. He wanted to return, however, his sudden return left him tired. Rest was not on his agenda, so ALBERT took a moment to re-energize his inner self by drawing energy in from the universe.

After a brief rest ALBERT called Mary who encourages him to come home." I agree with you, darling, I was wondering what the children had been up to anyway. My curiosity will speed up my trip home. See you in a few minutes".

Albert's trip home went quick and the children were at the landing dock to meet him.

Running to meet him Charles was full of excitement;" look, Dad. **PENNY** made her sound fairies and a dragon. Then I made them solid, so they wouldn't pop. I can control them with my thoughts and make them do stuff. Watch this! See how that small luminous dragon can swoop down from a beam when I call him.

Come Dragon. See he comes when I ask. **PENNY** can make anything. She can picture any animal in her mind. Then, I make them solid like I did the water in the pool. Cool huh"!

Albert looked at the children admiringly;" you kids sure are creative with your new abilities. Let's go see what the rest of the family has been up to today".

Mary hugged ALBERT and a little discretional playing; **ALBERT**, "you certainly had fun in your vision quest. Didn't you? Let's talk later. You know how **MYRA** has a quest for corporal immortality which has taken further steps towards all of us and our longevity. **MYRA** believes we can eliminate the disease of death any time soon. With her new ability, she was able to reach the answers much faster than they were progressing before yesterday".

"We are all progressing so quickly", Albert interjected; "this evolutionary shift is just as great as the paradigm shift the world went through in 2012. It took that shift to prepare us for this one. The world was not ready for the Gateway back then; it is ready now. We have to make a plan to share this with as many people as possible by July Fourth".

"**Yes dear!** I am sure the team at USE will come up with some way for everyone to have a chance to experience the Gateway. They have some of the best minds in the world working there along with all the resources that they need".

> **After dinner the children played while they did their chores. This would be another night of cosmic bliss for Albert and Mary, leaving Albert ready for his next day of excitement at the lab.**
>
> **Bill was there when Albert arrived at USE the next day;** "hi, ALBERT, the hospital held me overnight for observation. I feel great".
>
> "You look so much better. Why the extremely high spirit". "ALBERT, you know my old friend, Jenna? She came by to see me at the Center. We talked for hours. Then Jenna and I feel asleep in each other's arms. Jenna has always been my heartthrob. We really connected last night. We shared at a whole new level. Neither one of us will ever be the same".
>
> "I now realize and, I told this to Jenna, that it was thoughts of her that also brought me back yesterday. I told her she was better than venturing into a cosmic black hole. She took this as the compliment that I meant. Then she whispered to me that I just might get another opportunity to explore a cosmic black hole if she keeps coming around. I just blushed as we snuggled closer". (BILL finished with a happy sigh.)

Albert laughed;" that is funny. It sure sounds like you have found your twin flame. We always knew you two would find each other. You look wonderful together. Jenna and you are always so happy when you are around each other. For all of us that observed you both, neither of you ever seemed to notice".

Bill admitted;" sometimes I analyze everything too much, now I am realizing all that I missed by concentrating on one thing. My new experiences lately have taught me that going with the flow will allow for all the new experiences. Staying balanced or neutral expands my field of awareness. I cannot deny the connection I have with Jenna. I am grateful she feels the same way about me. How great is that"?

Giving Bill the thumbs up; "pretty great, my friend". "I know you are happy no matter what. However, it is always nice to share that happiness with others".

"BILL, there is so much for you to hear. I know I was in the city of Lemuria. See how the book by Anthony Hoggins shows the city, I was in the city of Lemuria". "Hoggins states that he has proof that he will reveal it further along in the book. In Chapter 10, I didn't find his proof. I haven't read any further yet today".

"If you want to keep reading Albert, I would like to study the Gateway a lot closer. I like the new name for the object, it is a fitting description. I was thinking of 'the Cosmic Library' only the Gateway is even better".

"Yes, the name fits into the USE Mission Statement and USE is the best value dispersers on the planet. So it will not take long for them to come up with a plan to share this with the world. Our team does not work with a marketing, profit driven paradigm anymore. They have long ago realized that truth, along with love, is the keys to spreading value". " Everyone benefits"!

> **Albert went back to reading and Bill attached the micro spectrometer to his visor to begin his examination. Starting at the top point of the Gateway, he made a thorough examination**

of every square inch. As he looked, he could feel himself being drawn into the sub-atomic micro universes making up the Gateway. He prepared himself for a new journey by watching his breathing and grounding himself by placing his feet firmly on the ground.

Meanwhile, Albert was on a separate vision journey back to the city of Lemuria. This time Albert was much more centered and felt he could get some answers.

Albert first noticed the savage, volatile world surrounding the city. Meteors were bombarding the surface of the planet but the city went unaffected. Large mastodons roamed in herds, many varieties of dinosaurs were just outside the city's borders. He saw insects the size of eagles and trees as large as small mountains encompassing acres for one tree.

ALBERT's mind chattered; these Lemuria guys must need constant supervision to protect them from this dangerous environment.

As ALBERT entered the outskirts of the city, he saw children playing in what appeared to be a school yard. The diversity of the children was like no other school he had ever seen before and they all played together without any apparent quarreling or bickering. Dealing with only loving vibrations must be the cause of such a wonderful atmosphere. ALBERT could feel the love coming from the children; they played together like an orchestra.

ALBERT's left brain thinking; language must be a huge barrier with all of this diversity. Without language their right brains must be working at peak levels and everything is communicated telepathically.

The buildings were tied together with stone pathways that had plush landscaping with exotic plants edging the walkways. Vegetable gardens were near each building along with fruit trees. Domestic animals roomed freely.

ALBERT came across what looked like the market place where he never saw any exchange of currency. Each location displayed the values they provided and some were full of wonder. In one display was a bunch of gem stones. ALBERT saw someone hold up a stone to the sunlight, where it blossomed into a flower of light particles with rainbow colors of intense beauty.

Up ahead, ALBERT noticed he was getting close to the location where he had encountered that voice that startled him on the previous visit. Now he felt prepared. He was becoming accustomed to the energy that was all around. Yet he felt his energy was unique and must be noticed. Just like before, his presence seemed to go un-noticed by everything and everyone.

Here, in the middle of a volatile world, was a place of peace, serenity and harmony. They created paradise, despite what is happening in the primitive surroundings, by uniting on the common denominator of love. Although the technology was being developed in a different way, he saw that in many ways they were far more advanced than mankind in ALBERT's reality. This was more the science of harmony, where development was guided by the heart-mind. Understanding and working with the universe was their genius.

All of the sudden, just like before, Albert hears a voice; "I see that you are back. Do not run away again, my friend".

ALBERT turned around and saw a large humanoid looking being standing over him that reached out and tenderly grabbed his hand. The spirit is luminescing with a calm vibration that could be felt. His antenna's moved about sensing reality on levels that our normal senses only begin to experience.

Albert remained calm although he asked a lot of questions "How is this possible"?

"How can we be having physical contact in a vision journey"?" No one up to this point has been able to even see me"!

"All of your questions will be answered in due time. I am Zeb of the Seventh Direction and we have been expecting you. This is not your second visit here, you have been here many times and we are old friends. You, old friend, are one of the universes greatest paradoxes ever known and as you and your family will see, your story has just begun".

How is it that we can communicate, Albert pondered?

Zeb answered as if Albert had asked out loud, "we are just outside their vibration or plain of existence. We comprehend each other because we are communicating on a level that is part of the universes harmonics. Your mind is doing the interpreting. Come with me and everything will reach clarity for you".

As Zeb and Albert traveled, they talked about existence. The universe is billions upon billions of years old, while existence is without any known time restrictions. There is no past, present or future. Everything just is. When you tap into source or prime creation, like you have done through the Gateway, you become aware of this limitlessness.

Zeb shared freely with Albert;" you can experience the continual creation of the whole of existence here, so do not let your rational mind limit or take control of you. Let everything unfold and use your rational mind to your advantage. Few of your species have made it here while they still had a corporal vessel to return to back "home". "You will take this back to the physical plain and attempt to explain what you have seen in a limited language. You will naturally fall short when attempting to convey everything".

"Consciously evolved beings have been part of existence all along while your species have only been around for a blink of an eye in the cosmic time stream. At the same time, you have been here all along. For you to be here is a mark of evolution for your species that few other life forms across the vastness have achieved. You are getting a small glimpse of just how vast and infinite everything really is".

ZEB continued; "as you are finding out in your visits to Lemuria, this is not the first time that your species has evolved to higher consciousness. Planet Earth is like a pineal gland for the universe. Its purpose is to continually bring new states of self-awareness to the prime consciousness. The development of Earth's inhabitants has been shaky at times and the outcome was inevitable. Your planet has been destroyed in many timelines, which just causes a cosmic re-boot where things are altered in the timeline that went wrong to bring about the desired result for the greater good of all. Earth is not the only pineal gland in the great "I am" yet she is a jewel and she/he is loved dearly".

"What you call the Gateway is part of a leap forward that was put into place by you, Albert. As you will see, this is just the beginning of your quest to help mankind. It was only fitting that you, with your family and friends, are the first to benefit from what you will set in motion. You are part of a purposeful temporal loop set into motion by you".

Albert asks;" why am I a part of this cosmic plan? How is this even possible"? ZEB continuing telepathically; "we are all part of something that we may not discover until the time is right. You created your own destiny in many ways. Your family and friends have major roles to play in the times ahead. I cannot reveal much more to you right now".

In the next moment, ALBERT was back in his lab. He looked over at BILL who looked like he was in a trance studying the Gateway. He went over and touched BILL on the shoulder. After a minute, BILL looked up at ALBERT saying,

"You have no idea what I have just gleaned. We are so limited in our knowledge, with so much to learn".

Both Albert and Bill wanted to share their vision journeys immediately. The intense excitement also brought a calming knowingness.

Bill started out saying; "we see what we want to see, we hear what we want to hear. We stop learning when we feel we know something. It is like a gravitational pull is taking place within our brain. Staying neutral and balanced eliminates the pull and activates the pineal gland, the all seeing eye". "We have poles in our head just like the planet and to evolve we experience pole shifts internally until we balance".

Bill stopped his narrative, being startled by a small noise. He turned and saw this mouse dressed in clothing peering at them from behind a desk leg.

"What's that I saw out of the corner of my eye? Come here, little one, we will not harm you".

The mouse stopped behind the leg of a desk and looked directly at BILL and ALBERT. He could not understand the words being spoken but he just felt the calming sincerity in the vibrations. He had never gotten this sincere an invitation from the gods before yet he remained cautious. With all the bravery he could muster, he stepped out from behind the leg of the desk and stood there like a knight expecting a challenge.

Albert (a little surprised) reassured his new acquaintance;" look, it is a mouse with clothes on it. Come here, little fellow".

The mouse puffed up his little chest and, with a confident stride like a conqueror, walked on two legs up to Bill and Albert squeaking and making hand gestures like he was making his demands known to all.

"I do not understand you, little guy, but I know someone who can".

Albert called home immediately;" **MARY,** bring **BRANDON** by the lab as soon as possible. Also bring **PENNY** and **CHARLES** as well. They are going to love the surprise we have for them".

CHAPTER 5

NEW FRIENDSHIPS

Mary brought Brandon, Penny and Charles to Albert's lab as he requested. They were delighted meeting this unsuspected visitor. The mouse was nervous seeing the new arrivals

ALBERT was able to calm his new little friend with just a look from his eyes and even though there was still a language barrier, a soothing contract was formed. The little mouse talked and talked or, should I say, squeaked and squeaked in a much calmer state of being.

Brandon spoke up right away; "I understand the mouse clearly".

The mouse realized this new communication bridge so he directed his attention to Brandon. "We have been leaving messages everywhere we go to let you know we are here. Message after message has been wiped up or overlooked. Not long ago, at our last location, we left droppings of poopy everywhere, that only made you angry. Then, you started to hunt us down. We follow the Oracle wherever it goes and now it is here. Besides, we had to leave or get away. It was the Oracle that told us to come here and wait its arrival. It arrived 3light cycles ago".

Brandon explained too his new little friend; "each age of light and dark are what we call days. It did arrive 3 days ago, as you say, and we are calling your Oracle, the Gateway".

"I am the one chosen by the tribe to go out and give the 'all clear' sign when you gods are not around", the mouse elaborated. "Lately I have been attempting to get your attention and cannot". "What is up with that"?

With an effort to give his friend a name Brandon asks; "so you are like the scout for your tribe"?

"Ya. That is what I said". "I am Scout for my family".

"The mouse's name is Scout. I've asked Scout if he would like everyone to understand him. Scout has agreed".

With that said, Brandon with his right hand index finger touched Scout on the left side of his head. A small spark of energy came from the tip of Brandon's finger.

In a squeaky high pitched voice, as clear as a bell.

"Oh, my Source! What was that? You Gods are powerful"!

"We are not gods, in the way you are referring to us", Mary chimed in. "Our connection with the great 'I am' is the same as yours, Mister Scout. Our size and capabilities do not make us superior. You are actually using more of your mind than we are. Even in our heightened state we have only tapped around fifty percent of our minds' potential, which is a giant leap. Not long ago, we used less than five percent of our minds".

In an effort to gather his wits Scout stopped Mary saying; "slow down pretty lady, Geez"! "Let's take one step at a time here. I do not know what a percent is. Why don't you quote me statistics, while you are at it"? "Percentage and statistics", "I have never had those concepts before now. What did you do to me? You are drawing me into your web"!

Penny started giggling; he is so cute. "I like him. Can we keep him"?

With an indignant tone in his voice scout replies; "hey there, little sister, nobody keeps me! I go where I choose". "You will have to win my heart and I play hard to get. Just because I have this cute little voice now and I am a fraction of your size, doesn't mean I am a push over". "FRACTION"!!

Scout continued looking at BRANDON. "Where did that come from"? "Is that like percentages"? "You really screwed me up, buddy boy. Fractions, percentages, statistics, concepts, what else did you do to me"?

Everyone was laughing, so Scout had to calm down.

Showing a bit of frustration; "so, this is funny to you! HUH! Oh well! They just don't get it".

Albert was still laughing with the others; "we understand more than you think, **SCOUT**. Wait until you hear about our old monetary system, then you can laugh at us".

Charles could not stop laughing. His contagious laughter set them all off again. "Do not worry, little friend, I will help you adjust to us".

Scout saw in CHARLES' eyes a kindred spirit and said with a bow; "I believe you can, my untainted one, oh Guardian of the playground".

> **Charles, Scout, Brandon and Penny all gathered to play; while Bill, Albert and Mary continued with their adult play by discussing their adventures of the day. The release of energy through laughter made for an interesting conversation.**
>
> **All were quiet as Albert shared his journey to Lemuria and his meeting with Zeb. His story made them feel that Zeb had reached a state of oneness with the universe and was like a gardener of consciousness.**

"We have to learn more about Zeb", Mary stated. "He has long ago ascended to where we are heading".

"Before we go further", Albert continued; "I would like to give you a summary of the Book **Chaos and Order.** It fits in with what we are learning".

"It took mankind realizing their true selves, shifting from the mind to the heart, realizing the power of self-determination, and getting past that threshold of self-destruction for the further growth of our species to continue". Do you remember all of the regulations of the self-absorbed governments, bankers, religions, big businesses who held themselves out as the higher authorities"? "Once the people became aware of this corporate agenda, the people realized that they could create a new reality that would benefit the whole of mankind instead of the few authorities".

"The veils of illusion that these controlling few erected over the history of man finally fell. The truth became clear to the masses".

"These self-absorbed, so called leaders brought no real value to mankind. Instead of helping others find their higher authority within, they set themselves up as the authorities, as a selfish means of control". "This mysticism that they used took advantage of everyone and had only their selfish intent to control. I am truly grateful that our human family chose to take that evolutionary step that lead not only to survival but also to prosperity".

Bill ponders out loud; "I remember"! "As long as people accepted their leaders' authority, the leaders had power. They used mis-direction, illusions, half-truths, persuasion, fear, coercion, propaganda and even mind control through media, education, programming and diet. We stand on the shoulders of those people that realized that truth; we became the conscious co-creators that we were meant to be".

Albert continued; "the change did not come easy". "I remember the resistance or struggle we had in integrating then releasing the learned knowledge and behaviors that was programmed into us starting at birth". "Many could not look outside the path they were corralled into, so the resistance did not start with the masses until their comfort level was threatened". "There are still many who do not see, understand or comprehend the changes continually taking place because they have a defined reality by placing limits on everything".

"The steps towards the Utopia we live in now rested in the individual's awareness of their own miracle of being, their self-worth, love, unity and common sense".

"**ALBERT**, my dear, you are rambling a little. We want to hear about **BILL**'s journey. Step ahead and give us the Nitti gritty."

"Let me finish with this", Albert added; "you all know where I was heading". "Evolution is about peaceful co-existence, pure intentions, gratefulness, allowance, forgiveness and balance. Oh yeah, when love and balance is equated into the solutions of every problem we leaped forward".

Bill stepped in; "an observation I made was that everyone needs to realize is we are all connected with everything. Your last comment about co-existence or co-creation being a guide or measuring stick for evolution is spot on".

"Not everything in the universe has a benefit at the time it is occurring. When a natural disaster occurs and things look bleak, it is hard to be grateful at the changes it will bring. Yet, even these experiences lead to better realities. We learn, then we make adjustments, so that when it happens again, we are much better prepared. Out of chaos 'if we learn', we get order".

"When I entered the micro universe, I could not help but notice that even in the sub-atomic universe there was a pattern of geometry to everything I experienced. At any given time we are all part of what looks like two interlocking eights, one being the micro, our true self, and the other being the macro. It even goes deeper than that. The vacuum which is the universe or multi verse is expanding inward much faster than it is expanding outward. What is so beautiful is that creation is a continuous non-stop, never pausing, the act of simply observing, creates. Everything seems to evolve following a unique numerology always doubling as each micro becomes the new macro as evolution keeps moving along. The numerology, I saw, was 0,1,2,4,8,4,2,1,0. What is so special about this is that the first 0 and last 0 occur simultaneously. Thus the end is also the beginning. No one or nothing ever dies it just evolves. I am not certain if I saw this because that is what I was expecting to see or that is just the way it was. I cleared my mind of all of my past pre-conceived universe. Much more came into clarity once I cleared my mind, as I witnessed the building blocks of the universe were actually universes on their own energy. Life was evolving even at this micro level and that evolution was affecting all the other things".

"The things that got out of balance would eventually burn up or extinguish it and that energy would disperse into the mix without getting lost. The micro universe that kept its own geometric balance seemed to be eternally healthy".

"There was space between all particles of matter, the smaller I got the larger the space between the matter got and the matter looked like galaxies and solar systems with suns, planets, moons". 'Everything had its own source/connection with the great 'I am'.

"I got so small that I entered a planet with inhabitants and the possibility of sub-sub-atomic worlds, which became increasingly more possible. This could go on for infinity". "Is it possible that we are just a sub-atomic universe within something much bigger"? "With everything I observed or witnessed, the reality that I was studying in the Gateway did not leave me. I felt it was time to return. I made several other observations on my way back".

"The universes that held their geometric shapes put out a harmonic vibration that is what we feel when we allow ourselves to feel pure unconditional love.

That is the best way I can describe it. Also the vibrational scale seemed to have mathematical proportions that would probably take a while to figure out. Then, the thought that there were trillions upon trillions of possible sub-atomic universe inside everything we observe is a mind boggler".

"I also noticed that when something happened, while I was observing the sub-atomic inhabitants, say, they reached a new enlightenment or something like that, it would send out a pulse into the connecting pathways that lead to everything. I observed a large part of their history even though I was only there for a few moments".

"As I got larger, I was able to see what these pulses looked like and how they appeared as light energy, illuminating the pathways. It was spectacular to witness. However, as I grew larger, it became less apparent. The geometry became clear once again. Then I was back, looking at the Gateway".

"Everything is connected and remains its own individual at the same time. If we recognize our individuality, we should also recognize our connections. Our true uniqueness is in our perceptions". "We all perceive differently thus no one's experience is ever the same. Man has evolved to where we are conscious co-creators. "It took a long while for us, as a species, to realize our co-dependence with not only each other but also the planet, the universe and the prime creation".

"Our species, as conscious co-creators, have to take into consideration 'what we take we have to give back". "We cannot cut down trees without planting new ones. Our actions/interactions between us, within us, with nature and the universe are signs of our evolution. Our actions expose our intent". "So far we have our awareness of our own existence, of existence itself, of co-existence; our awareness of creation and co-creation. These are all great leaps in consciousness. We are about to make another great leap with the Gateway, when we introduce it to the world".

Mary nodded in agreement; "that is so true". "Even before my ability to read minds or hear what others were thinking, I knew that what we **think** is a form of creation or prevention from us creating anything. All that we do or not do, starts within us". "It takes motivation and action to get anything done. Desire to better our lives is a major motivation in all we do. We have learned throughout history what motivates people. Then we had to learn to consider everything around us in our decision to take action. Even a single cell moves towards nutrition and avoids harm".

"The ability to look at the effects of our actions is leaded us to find out that love should be the advisor within. Love is the key to co-existence. Love will lead us towards nutrition. Yet love is mis-understood by so many people. Our body's biological reactions to each other have been mistaken for love. A strong belief that we need someone to be happy is mis-taken for love".

Mary started reminiscing; "so what is love"? "To me, love is acceptance, allowance, forgiveness, gratitude with pure, honorable intent. First, we learn to love ourselves unconditionally, then others, then nature and then the universe". "So loving is another sign of evolution within the universe. With love we learn and make co-existence possible. With love guiding our actions, then our interactions will be for the greater good of all. Our connection with one another should only make us grow".

"Maybe this is why not everyone is affected by the Gateway. Maybe their ability to love is hampered by their interpretation of love. They may be self-absorbed, believing that they are the ones with the answers".

Adding comment, Albert replies; "we and the people like us are the first to admit that we do not know anything, 'Even with the universe unfolding before our eyes, right in front of us, revealing things never seen before by any of us". "Actually this only confirms how little we know. All of our answers just lead to more questions".

Bill picked up the thread of his journey into the micro universe; "here's another point about evolution about man's ability to ask questions, you may recall, I had progressed very far in this capacity. Everything I held made me wonder and needed to be observed, openly for continual comprehension".

"Everything has a singularity and is part of a greater singularity. An atom contains an entire universe, like our own, full of singularities".

"On my way back, I thought I saw a glimpse of me on my way into that universe. I wanted to tell myself to go further. As you know, that did not happen. I can now see why not everyone is ready for the Gateway. They are going to have to have the ability to handle what they see and if they are stuck on one belief then denial will not let them except anything new. There is more to existence than anyone could possible imagine. It seems like an experiment of highly evolved, super-advanced species. We could be being observed, like a sample in a Petri dish in their lab. From what we have seen lately, nothing would surprise me".

Mary shared her thought once more; "the theory of the singularity or primeval atom and the big bang that created our ever expanding universe makes this universe finite. What kind of mind boggling vastness could contain the whole micro and macro-universe? Are there other universes forming in this vastness? Are we capable of comprehending all that there is? It is exciting to be a part of something so grand, even if we are but a tiny piece of it all. At least, we can feel our connection to it. This brings us to another sign of evolution and that is the realization of everything's connection to prime creation".

In summary Albert added; "finding common denominators is one of our greatest learning tools. We need all the tools we have to create, this does not mean that mass agreement is a sign of validity; it just means that there are answers we can all grasp being worded differently". "We have discussed many common denominators in our conversations, yet even this conversation is based on past knowledge and perceptions. Our left brains are putting things into logical perspectives so we can deal with them. This is a path towards understanding and a way for us to keep our sanity. The left brain is kind of a safety mechanism that helps us create. We are integrating our new experiences with past data".

"So we are looking at things with a pre-conceived notion and interpreting events in ways we can relate to them. That means that there is so much more we are missing, because it does not fit into our realm of reasoning".

Mary adds; "it seems as though we are still limited no matter how far we progress. That is humbling, yet empowering at the same time".

The children and Scout had been listening in on this conversation since Bill started speaking.

"We make up our own rules in our own playground, Daddy".

With a grin of pride Albert turns to Charles; "from the mouth of youth comes the summary of individual existence". "Yes, Charles, we make our own rules in the playground and if we let others make the rules for us, then you can almost bet that they will make the rules so only they can win. It took mankind a long time to discover what you know instinctively. Control tactics disappeared when we figured this one concept out".

"The golden rule of do unto others as you would have them do unto you, or bring no harm, guides the rules of the playground, Charles".

CHAPTER 6

SPREADING THE WISDOM

The family stayed around all afternoon at the lab. The day went on with play and good conversation. Then, it came time for everyone to return home. Mary and the children left before Albert. Bill left soon after them. Albert said his goodbye to Scout, when he closed up for the evening.

Scout returned to his **tribe** full of anticipation; "you will find this hard to believe what happened with the gods and I".

One of his fellow mice Manny asked; "what are they like"? "How could they talk with you"? "Why are you still alive"? "Come on, everyone, what do you say"?

"We have bridged a tremendous gap today", Scout started. "The humans have reached a new understanding of us and I have a new understanding of them. All that it took was looking at each other from a different perspective. My new friends are very open, not like the ones we have dealt with before this time. The young ones are very receptive and full of love".

"The hu-manes are excited about meeting the rest of us. I promised to bring you with me on the next age of light which they call daytime. The one child called **BRANDON** will help us with our communication gap. I can now speak with them and I understand what they are saying. They have strange concepts that come with this new ability to communicate. After a while, you will get used to it. It is confusing at first".

Babbler, known for his babbling; "how do we trust them"? "Our whole history is full of the abuse they have perpetrated on our kind. The Humanes have used us in experiments, hunted us down, poisoned us en-mass, kept us as pets, chased us with sticks and treated us with fear, dishonor, and inferior standing".

"They treat each other the same way", Scout explained. "However, not all of them are like this. I found out today that they have been going through an evolution just like we have. The hu-manes have just learned to get along with each other by focusing on their common denominators instead of their differences. We are not dealing with the same heartless godlike beings anymore. First thing that we have to remember is that they are not gods in the way we think of them. We have the same god within us also. We are just as much a part of Prime Creation as anything else".

"Once again, it is about changing our perspective. We need to let go of our past to embrace the present. Let go of our pre-conceptions. We will have to be brave to do this. We will have to think new thoughts, see more of the bigger picture with an open frame of reference".

A voice from the back of the tribe (Jasmine) could be heard; "they have affected you, **SCOUT**". "Look at our **TRIBE**, **SCOUT**. You are not the same as when you left at the last light cycle. You have brought back with you new knowledge as well as a ray of hope. I would love to walk with you on your next journey with the hu-manes".

Jasmine walked up and linked her arm into SCOUT's; "so, who else is with us? Are we mice or fleas"?

Cheezer stepped forward asking; "will we get some cheese out of this meeting"? "If they share their cheese, then you can count me in".

CHEEZER took SCOUT's other arm into his then watched as most of the others stepped forward linking arms. BELCHER, MENDER, RUNNER, CRACKER, BELL, DAZZLER and even SQUEAMISH, all agreed to go with Scout on the next age of light.

SCRIBE, WISDOM, PROVIDER, CHAKRA, DANCER and GARDENER also joined the group. This was to be like the real first contact with a species that had been here all along and the Wisdom Keepers had to come along.

Babbler finally stepped up; "if all of you are going, then so am I. I cannot believe we are doing this, who is to say that we are not walking into a trap. That would be just like the hu-manes to trap us with kindness. Here we go again, trusting the hu-manes. How soon we forget. I want some of that cheese too so I will go. Whatever will be, will be"!

"Relax, Babbler", Scout reassured. "This is nothing like we have dealt with before".

The next morning at Albert's and Mary's habitat, Albert is leaving for work.

"What a beautiful day to go to work", Albert announced. "**MARY**, please bring the children by later. I just want to get an early start at work so I can finish reading the Hoggins' book. I sure can't wait to get the answers hidden in that book. This mystery has to be solved to proceed safely with the great sharing that was to take place soon on this planet. See you all later. Love ya".

The ride to USE went smooth as usual, this was an early arrival for Albert although Bill was already hard at work.

"I had to come in early to get through Hoggins' book. I am so excited about it and what can be discovered".

Excited about a new idea, Bill says; "I want to work on planning another journey into the multi-universes. This journey is to go back to the creation of the universe, if that is even possible. I envision all of our group accompanying me on this journey. **MARY** will help link our minds".

"**MYRA** is on her way over. I hope Scout would come along also. Let me get to work on the details of setting the vision quest while you read".

Albert went back to reading and mumbling aloud; "Anthony Hoggins sure has such a flamboyant way of describing everything. I can't get through a chapter without taking one of my trips into the time stream".

> It was easy to visualize Hoggins' descriptions even for someone without **ALBERT**'s abilities. Hoggins talked about Lemuria as the founding city, even before Samaria or Atlantis. In the book, Anthony tells how the city of Lemuria still existed to this day while a millennia ago the whole city rose from the ground to travel into the stars. They left behind emissaries to help guide mankind in its development.
>
> The bloodlines of these emissaries are in the DNA of many living persons today. No records of this is evident to the casual observer and even the emissaries lost contact with Lemuria over time. Only mental visions or dreams connected the emissaries to their heritage which was also meant to be mankind's heritage. Not all the emissaries left behind agreed with each other, so a division took place soon after Lemuria left.
>
> Some of the emissaries felt they were left behind on this mud ball of a planet so they set about making things as comfortable for themselves as possible, no matter what the outcome for the rest of civilization. This small group became the controllers

of the world by eliminating the rest of the emissaries and keeping common knowledge from everyone else.

It became the sole purpose of these dark ones to create an illusion of need and dependence from the masses, who could not find answers on their own, to the dark ones as they held themselves up as the higher authorities. They discouraged and trampled those individuals that showed the capacity to think or evolve on their own.

These few emissaries plunged mankind into the Stone Age, where they could develop man to serve the emissaries. They knew that if man remembered who they were, where they came from, their connection with the universe and what they were capable of achieving the emissaries would not be served, so knowledge was hidden and history was written to suit the needs of the dark ones.

Force, fraud, repression, illusion, starvation, fear, war, destruction, division and coercion became the tools of this dark cabal. Protocols were set up for the dark ones' lineage to follow that would eventually lead to the complete control of the planet and the inhabitants.

However, nothing was going as planned for this planet Earth and the emissary's dark designs. Their battle was harder than they anticipated because every child born has the knowledge of who they are at birth.

The dark ones had to keep repressing that knowledge. Many of the good emissaries kept returning to this Third Dimensional plain and bringing reminders to the populace.

Programming with false propaganda started at an early age. People were only taught enough to make them a valued slave to the dark cabal. As more people saw through the illusions, they were eliminated or, in the least, discriminated against by others. Even language was used to divide and conquer. Many different religions were formed, which encouraged people to fight about whose god was correct. Any enlightenment was twisted, ridiculed, buried or stifled in some way. Fear of each other was played like a fine tuned fiddle. Most people fell right in line fully unaware of these manipulations.

Most of the followers did so under the illusion that they were doing the right thing for their people and their rulers. Even a lot of the rulers, kings, emperors, religious leaders and royalty were just pawns for the protocols of the few in the dark cabal. Stimulate dependency and then take things away. This was another tool effective in gaining control. Alcohol, drugs, currency, fuels, energy, food, water and many other things were tools to create dependency that either made one complacent or, by controlling the substance, you could control the people.

Who cares who is president or monarch, if they are being controlled from behind the scene? Give the people an illusion of choice, while we operate undisclosed agendas behind the curtain. Keep them occupied with games and trivia, while we proceed on with our intent. These people that have this imaginary control stifle genius, stifle knowledge, stifle change, stifle self-determination and self-worth. If we, the people, let them!

Still the truth kept showing up in everything for those that choose to see. The veils of illusion cannot hold back a truth seeker. The answer is in the ability to create on your own, detached from what other are creating as well as your creations. Only give your consent or validation towards helpful/positive intent or value.

Albert started musing to himself; I relate to all I'm reading because I remember the fall of the cheaters or as Anthony Hoggins called them, the dark cabal. First, I remember everyone getting together in small groups, then the groups started getting together. People started thinking with their hearts. Those that chose greed over love were cast to the side to deal with each other. The cheating ways were disclosed. Those that participated were shamed, forgiven and offered repentance. Those that did not repent were allowed to live, only they no longer held any sway or influence over anyone else. For them, it was like being out of phase with the rest of the world. Most of these diehard tyrants found each other and still live in their depravity.

The real change happened when value producers and value creators were finally in control of their own lives and mankind quickly blossomed. The new society was the people and it takes a whole tribe to raise a child. Education changed as children were encouraged to find that spark of happiness in what they love to do then develop this into a value for all. Children were given answers as well as encouraged to seek more answers on their own. The teachers returned to what they love to do, TEACH!

I'm sure that Anthony's book was withheld from circulation as it revealed so much. That is probably why there were so few copies available. There isn't much more information about the Gateway except that mankind was not ready for it yet and Anthony knew this. Wow, that is a mouthful.

> **As ALBERT marked his page and closed the book, his mind was racing with new questions. He had been in the middle of the chaos created by the last ditch efforts of the cheaters to hold on to their illusion of control, of power. They did not give in easily and they tried to cause as much disorder as they could. If not for the geniuses that came out to spearhead a new paradigm, things would have gotten worse. These loving geniuses were able to bring about an awareness of how life could be and allow everyone to become the people they were meant to be as well as the miracles that they were already.**

People became detached from the illusionary power structure by thinking on their own and coming up with new ways to interact with each other. The masses were now unencumbered by the unnecessary stress that was forced upon them by the now defunct power mongers. The consumer made sure that the quality of goods received required no exchange or return, thus leaving a throwaway wasteful society in the past.

Licensing, insurance, money, banking, language, contracts, treaties, Constitutions, Trusts, service as well as history was being re-worked for the common good. The profit driven paradigm was becoming a dogma of the past. When something is broken or in error and we know as well as have everything we need to make the repair or correction: it becomes our duty to do so.

New energy sources became available that allowed people to remove themselves from the controlling grid. Fossil fuels were slowly replaced with new technology as it became available. Mankind was now free to develop rapidly.

What happened to Anthony? Will we ever know?

MARY arrived with the children all excited to meet Scout's friends. "Children, help **SCOUT** feel it's safe to bring out his brave **TRIBE**. **CHARLES,** contain your excitement. You'll meet more of the mice tribe".

Penny blew a bubble; "**SCOUT,** here is a soap bubble for you". "Yep, it looks just like you".

Charles proudly adds; "I made the bubble harden so the molecules wouldn't pop or frighten your **TRIBE** and our new little friends".

"Hi BRANDON, PENNY and CHARLES", Scout welcomes. "Come on, family, no need to be so timid. Come out and meet my new friends, the hu-manes".

Brandon asked as kindly as possible; "sweet, gentle friends, let me touch each of you on your left temple. It will not hurt and we can then talk with each other".

They all agreed to allow this to happen. Brandon started by touching Babbler first which set of a Barrage that was not expected.

The rambling started when he was touched; "what did you do to us? How did you do that? What are you going to do next? Should I run? I mean, should we run? Of course, I would not leave you guys behind. Do you have any cheese? That was part of my deal to come out here! Where are your sticks and poison? Don't put me in your experiment".

"Calm down, **BABBLER**", Scout said to help his friend. "They are not going to harm us".

Scout turned to MARY and pleaded; "could you, please, find us some cheese for our **TRIBE**"?

"I brought you some cheese". Since this stuff is not good for you, I also brought a cut up fruit".

Albert assured the brave mouse tribe; "do not be afraid of us, little ones. We are grateful for our new friendship and you are very courageous for trusting us. We have much to learn from each other".

Belligerently shaking his fist, Babbler rambles; "we can teach you a thing or two, that's for sure. What is wrong with you hu-manes? Did someone beat you with a meanness stick"?

Scout calms Babbler before he could get started; "this is a fresh start, **BABBLER**. Put all of that behind you; do not carry your past experiences forward with you. Things have changed so we cannot bring our old thoughts with us into this new world".

Wisdom back Scout up by adding; "we will open our hearts to those that are worthy with a bit of caution. I sense a higher vibration with these hu-manes and that we have nothing to fear. The legendary time of unity foretold by our ancestors is upon us and **SCOUT** is leading us to the beginning of the path. We should see where this path will lead us".

Scribe mouse was mumbling loudly as he scribbled on his pad. "There will be songs written about this time and sung from now forward. These songs will be the tales of the bold tribe that blazed the path for others to follow".

Albert spoke to all the mice. "This is a much bigger occasion than you may all realize. We hu-manes, as you call us, are on a path of discovery also that we want to share with those of you who so choose to join us. You have already benefitted from the effects of what we call The Gateway. So you know it will not harm you. We plan on sharing it with the world. You are welcome to join us".

Jasmine grabbed SCOUT's arm for support. "what you call The Gateway, we have named The Source Enhancer and some call The Spirit Guide or Oracle. We have guarded it for many generations".

Bravely stepping forward, Scout accepts Albert's offer. "As guardians of The Source Enhancer or Oracle we will join you on your path. May this day go down in micetory".

Charles blurts out; "so let the fun begin. What are we planning on doing"?

> **For the next couple hours, they all reviewed the 4th of July plan that was being developed. The scope and intent of the plan was amazingly simple. The goal was to share with the world a discovery that mankind had prepared for during their evolution.**

Towards the end of the day, Albert suggest; "it's almost time to go to our home, so let us test the limit of our new abilities by going on a quest for the creation of the universe. Bill thought we could make this trip together. **MARY**, can you bring the children back tomorrow to form a link with everyone to go on this journey together"?

"**ALBERT**, we wouldn't miss it", Mary agrees. "It will be interesting to get different perspectives on what we witness. Be sure to come home early for dinner, darling".

CHAPTER 7

NEW AND OLD CREATIONS

The next day at the lab, everyone was there. The room was vibrating with excitement while everyone listened to Bill review his thoughts for the journey.

"In reviewing these plans to accompany **ALBERT** on his vision journey to the source or the beginning of the universe, it is important we understand certain points. The scientists have calculated the age of the universe many times and they keep making it older. So if the trigger for our journey takes us right there, like it has in **ALBERT**'s past visions, then the age of the universe will not matter. The trouble is nobody has actually seen the creation of the universe, so all we have is theories and speculations based on observations".

Bill continued; "the big bang theory of the expanding universe is widely accepted but it is just a theory. What if the universe is just growing, like how we grow from childhood to adults? What if we are part of a conscious cosmic entity that exists among billions of other entities, like I experienced in the micro universe only outward"?

"Another encounter we may have is determining where the beginning is or what constitutes the beginning. Usually in the circle of life, the beginning of anything is the end of something else".

"It is better not to speculate, so our consciousness cannot create what we expect to see. Wherever we end up, **MARY** is our anchor to each other. She will always have to remain linked to you and if you lose that link, find someone close to you and link with them. Our physical bodies are not in any danger yet we need to return to them".

Scout was dancing around in frustration that he might not get heard. "We have to go back in leaps because you know what **now** looks like. We can observe the changes. Even if we determine there is no true beginning we can see the progression of things. As the **scout** for my **TRIBE**, I know that you have to check things out slowly, observe your surroundings, move forward with caution and remember your path back to safety. We will need, what you call, the Gateway to make this journey out and to return safely. The Gateway is a gift from the first species ever to reach the cosmic connection to the source and travel the stars. They now exist in non-ordinary reality that we visit in our minds".

A little stunned by Scouts observations, Bill continues. "You sure learned a lot in these few years, **SCOUT**. It will be interesting to see if we all experience the same thing or will it be different for each of us? In our first experiment with the Gateway we all seemed to be there and our experiences were all different according to our uniqueness. Now we have a defined purpose that may be challenging. I am sure our uniqueness will have its affect. It is said that things change simply by observing. The act of observation makes the change so you never see anything in its actual state of being."

With a bit of concern, Mary suggest;" it is very important that we do not take any pre-conceived thoughts with us on this journey. The children have an advantage and we all have that childlike mind. We will have no problem by remembering that mind. We should all have a good lunch before we do anything".

While at lunch they discussed further preoperational plans with Bill.

Bill continued telling about his journey into the micro-universe; "As I got smaller, I noticed that the particles in the atom we call protons, electrons and neutron and even smaller ones we call quarks or the constituents of baryons and mesons moved at an alarming rate of speed and collisions with other particles occurred continuously".

"Collisions are what make up every new creation. Collision and reproduction by controlled collision. Collisions happen all around us all the time, like the wind colliding into the trees, the ocean colliding with the beach, light colliding into dark, the sperm colliding with the egg and so on. Most results are typical only some cause change or creation we cannot perceive. Yet with what appears to be chaotic actions has an unbelievable geometric order on all levels of existence as if guided by purposeful consciousness; a consciousness to which we all belong".

We are going to be a collision of our unique consciousness with the universe and we do not know the effects we may have, simply by observing. As beings of pure conscious energy colliding with the unknown, we could have affect that may change the course of all development from here on out".

"This should not deter us from making our journey", Albert added. "As long as we hold the positive love vibration that is natural in every one of us, we will only bring uplifting change. As you said, **BILL**, there is order to the universe and so what we do is part of a divine plan".

"I think we should make this happen when we finish our lunch. Too much pondering is not going to help with the new comprehensions we may encounter".

Mary suggests; "we should all meditate and do a clearing before this journey begins. In this way, we are already in tune with the universe when we start. One of us needs to stay behind to act as an anchor to this reality".

"I will volunteer to stay behind", Myra agrees. "I will be with you in many ways and you can all share with me when you return. I have a strong tie with **MARY** so you will all be safe".

> They all sat in a circle around the Gateway holding hands or paws and meditating. When they opened their eyes, MYRA started the Gateway spinning, for only a brief moment the vortex that was created by the Gateway took on the shape of a double strand DNA looping back into itself. It then it quickly went to many strands looping back to the Gateway that expanded so quickly that it took on the shape of the universe. This happened so fast that they almost did not see it.
>
> The first leap took them to a point where planet Earth was just forming and was being bombarded by meteors of all sizes and shapes each bringing with it a unique quality that will lead to the development of life on Earth. This was the beginning of bringing order to this section if this solar system. Many other systems have already formed within the Milky Way Galaxy with life forms in some areas that are already advanced millions of years.
>
> As if he had been with them the whole time, everyone heard a voice that only Albert recognized.

Like a shared thought, Zeb communicated with all the adventurers at once. "I see that the intent of all here is to come up with answers that have perplexed man for some time. Keep in mind that even this is but a fraction of what is, here, where time has no limits, you can learn many things. Think of this as a library, where you can find answers on any subject, except to cover the whole library would take forever. New knowledge is uncovered continuously and added to the archives".

"I will guide you to the answers you seek and how far we go is up to you. I hear your thoughts as you hear mine in your mind. **ALBERT**, I see you have met **SCOUT** and brought with you many new friends that I can tell you have a tremendous role in things to come."

"I will lead the group to a place where the universe could be observed from an outside perspective. As you travel, the universe will appear to get smaller. When you arrive in the macro-universe you may observe that the universe looks like a peeled transparent tangerine. Everything is looped out from the source seed and back like the DNA loop you observed when The Gateway was first activated on this journey. Each loop was separate and connected by what looked like neural pathways like in our brains. Some of you have coined the name taurus fields and that we live in a taurus garden. This is an accurate insight that begins a whole new realm of perception".

You could feel a universal consciousness that you now realize mankind was part of, realizing the cosmic healing that the universe must have gone through before mankind started to awaken on a global scale. Our irresponsible self-destructive ways must have been like an illness to the harmony of cosmic conscious existence.

They were dumbfounded at the vastness that was capable of encompassing our entire universe.
"AWESOME….."

In wonder, Penny spoke out; "look, see all the glowing orbs out in the massive vastness of that void. What …".

Zeb answered her before she could ask;" this universe, you call home, is just one of an infinite number of other universes. They all have their own beginning and are all connected by what you are referring to as the void field. Each one has wonders that rival the wonders of your universe, the uniqueness of our universe. Each one is also a part of a much larger macro-universe that goes on for infinity. That is a journey for another time".

"Observe how everything in our universe gets smaller and smaller as you watch. All time exist in the now. This traveling is like going upstream in a river. Reverse collisions are happening at an alarming rate. It is like watching a rainfall in reverse where the water rises up into the clouds as droplets then separate into smaller particles that are formed from evaporation".

"The universe is collapsing into itself, condensing to a smaller and smaller version of itself. You can feel the vast unity consciousness going through changes just like a child goes through as they grow to adulthood". "Isn't that right, **CHARLES**"?

"Notice the universe is getting as small as the point of a pin where a rift or tear in the fabric is making up the void that appeared into which the now tiny universe disappeared".

"You could follow your universe into the rift. This will take you on a whole new sojourn; however you may have a hard time returning. As you can see, there is no true beginning or end, just change. Time is infinite in each direction just like space".

"This is where we should head back", Albert relays. "All of our answers open up thousands of more questions which we all find exhilarating, only it appears that knowledge is just as vast as time and space."

"How pleasantly humbling it makes you feel," Mary shares. "The universe exists within each of us and we also exist in the universe, just like the universe exist within the macro-universe". "WOW"!!

With a little laugh Bill says; "from what we just observed our universe did not begin with a big bang, it was much more like the conception of a child that grew into adulthood. Maybe if we went into the rift, we would have witnessed the big banging"?

The adults (including Zeb) all laughed at this, while the children and the mice did not catch the humor.

"What did **BILL** mean by that", Charles asks?

Even telepathy cannot convey certain concepts.

Mary answers aloud in a kind voice; "the answer will come when you are ready for it, Charles".

"This is where we part ways my friends", Zeb announces. "Even I can still find humor in everything so keep your spirits high".

Next, they were all back in their bodies and stretching out. SCOUT and his TRIBE were all quiet as mice with blank expressions on their faces.

Myra was getting worried thinking; maybe they could not take what they had experienced. Will they be alright? Look one is stirring….

Babbler started rambling; "you know, I do not know what just happened. Can we go back? Never in my recollection could I even imagine seeing what we saw. How do we even think we are special when there is so much more? What a ride we are on. This is all so cool"!!

Scout grinned; "we are glad you are alright, **BABBLER**. Now that we cannot hear your thoughts, please keep those lips silent".

Jasmine started laughing; "your babbling mind was a funny distraction on the journey. You must have a hard time keeping it all inside sometimes".

CHARLES, BRANDON and PENNY were all relieved to see the mice become conscious and started laughing at the show they put on calming BABBLER down.

The atmosphere in the lab upon returning was full of love and laughter as they all gave an account of their experience one by one. The account of what happened did not vary much from one to the other.

However, SCOUT's observations had a unique perspective that made ALBERT comprehend and appreciate what ZEB had said about the influence these new friends would have in the times ahead.

"We have never seen much outside of our boxes or hiding holes. When we experience something new it was usually with fear of the unknown. We had little comprehension of anything that was not right in front of us, yet we took a journey to a source of constant creation. This would have driven us insane if we approached this journey in our normal fear mode".

"Our new relationship with you, hu-manes, has allowed us to approach new directions with curiosity, love and lightheartedness. These new paradigms are only latent emotions repressed by fear and are now free to be felt. This showed me that what we see is affected by what we feel and so connected to our emotional baggage. So instead of becoming a basket case, we were able to process things in a different light and come out of it happy, full of life and stronger than ever. Our fear was the wedge that held back our evolution. Once we removed it, we have leaped into the realization of the universe group consciousness. This is one heck of a leap for us and yet we survived it, we are stronger because of it and we are ready for more. I have never felt so powerful and insignificant at the same time, even though now I realize that nothing is insignificant".

> **The account of the journey for SCOUT was the same as the others and he was glad the hu-manes went first so he could learn more of the language or terminologies they used. Listening to them gave all the mice a new understanding of what they had just experienced.**

Albert started a summary of the events; "the universe seems to have been created out of an act of love and we have to return to that love vibration to bring growth and become one with creation. Of course, this is based on what we experienced on our vision journey. We are just attempting to comprehend it by giving description. There is no duality in the universe; this is something we, hu-manes, made up. Even what we consider the most devastating occurrences, brings about an even newer creation with the combined characteristics of the collision. The heart center leads us to the right answers because this is where we originate and where our connection is to creation".

Listening intently, Myra gratefully adds; "thank you all for sharing your path with us. I see the universe is just like us when we are born, pure of learned behavioral patterns, beliefs or habits, pure with love and trust. The growth of the universe is tied to all that inhabit it like a field or web. Our consciousness affects all consciousness. We are the miracle of billions of years of evolution and change and, even to this day, we are the biggest hope and greatest threat for continued survival. May our new experiences bring new, never seen before, creations to life"!

> **That evening was full of excitement as this day's events was all recorded and being broadcast around the world. The mice became overnight sensations without a clue that this was happening or the results it would bring. All they were concerned about was telling the rest of the tribe their story and resting for the night.**

The celebrity spotlight would prove to be more of an adventure than any of the journeys; showing them all that there is still much to learn in the ordinary reality of the group consciousness.

The next day would change the lives of our whole cast of characters and a giant step to world unity on a level unimaginable in previous dogmas. The earth had a new vibration and spectrum in its glow that was felt and seen throughout the cosmos like a refreshing burst of energy.

CHAPTER 8

PREPARATIONS BEGIN

The now celebrity group met again the next day in the recording studio to announce plans for the coming world event introducing the Gateway to everyone who chooses to listen.

ALBERT IS giving his summary on a morning telecast that is available to the world.

Albert; "I wish to introduce our whole team of researchers, including our new friends, **SCOUT** and several members of his **TRIBE**. The Gateway is like a quantum computer that stores all the combined knowledge of existence. The holographic image of the universe is just the opening page to accessing any of this knowledge. We also have this knowledge within us. The affect it had on us all brought out our latent characteristics that already existed within us. These enhanced abilities are dormant within us all. They are brought out by exposure to the activated Gateway. The Gateway helps you enhance the ability of tapping into our own universal data stream".

"Our guide, **ZEB**, told us that we were in a cosmic library where he was acting as the librarian that will show you where to access what you want. All of this knowledge you already have within you and even the Gateway's massive data storage does not include the amount of knowledge we have access from within our own heart/mind".

"The Gateway taps into the sources within us in such a way that allows the answers to come to us. When I made my journey to ancient Lemuria, I was asking the specific question about the creation of the Gateway. The answers are there and I just need to find them. This journey is chronicled for those that want to review it along with all of our experiences from the moment the Gateway arrived here at *USE Intergalactic Trust*".

"There are many of you that are not ready for this step in your evolutionary journey and you will probably not experience the activation of the Gateway. It may appear as a great light show and nothing more. Please enjoy the light show taking with you the benefit of a smile and a ouhh-ahhh. The ones that are ready can rest assured that this will not only elevate you to the next path that you wish to travel but it will also enhance your personal essence".

"We have a plan to bring this to as many people across the planet who wish to take part in this great sharing, however, you have to go to the nearest location to you or your favorite place on the schedule, which will be announced shortly by our *USE* planning council".

"Each experience will be truly unique at every location as well as for every individual. We will follow the lay lines from East to West as much as possible having events at geometric node locations to help Mother Earth and let Mother Earth help us".

"Several teams will be formed to take off for different locations with the main event being scheduled to last 5 minute. Believe me when I say, that 5 minutes is plenty in a timeless journey. The events leading up to or following the main event will also be full of excitement as you will be fed a live stream of each event. In this way, you can see how change is taking place and watch cosmic history in the making".

"The Gateway will be teleported from one location to the other with our teams traveling on the sonic bullet train. All of the details are being worked out and as things develop we will continue informing you. This has never been done before, where the whole planet is included in one day's celebration. Just the act of global unity is an accomplishment on its own".

"Some may say that this is an artificial way of reaching what we are already capable of doing. This is true in many ways. The same thing could be said about many other technologies and even books, which are tools used to help us evolve. For those individuals that have ascended on their own and move freely with the cosmic energy field, we could use your help as anchors, guides, messengers, interpreters, watchers and any other capacity you choose. This is a leap for mankind into the vastness of non-ordinary reality".

"Many of you, Ascended Masters, have been helping us all along knowing the course and potential of each one of us as to whom we are meant to become. As individuals we can harmonize with the universe. Now we are doing it as a species. Our love vibration will echo to the far reaches of the universe bringing about a cosmic healing of unimaginable proportions. This will give back to the Creator what it has given to us freely as co-creators".

"Only the great paradigm shift of 2023 and 2024 compares with what we are bringing to mankind today or the disclosure and unveiling of truth that happened at that same time. Co-creators were ready for that cosmic shift and I believe we are ready for yet another monumental step for humanity".

"We had best honor our benefactor's gift to humanity by sharing it with everyone. I hope to see you at one of our stops and wish you all the love in the world".

"Now I have the pleasure of introducing my family of pioneers including our new friend, **SCOUT**, who boldly changed his own and his **TRIBE**'s inbred, well deserved, fears of us by stepping into the unknown".

> **SCOUT was not sure what was going on. He had seen the moving pictures on walls and even holographic images from a distance before only this was always considered the power of the hu-manes. So he never understood when he saw his image on the screen. He thought it was another mouse that was mimicking his movements and speech; so he got defensive.**

Albert explained; "SCOUT, that is a projection of you. You **may not know** what is going on but you can take advantage of this new circumstance by venting your anger with kind, strong words of acceptance with caution. Many will hear you".

Scout started speaking his thoughts; "the universe is present in everything. My **TRIBE**'s existence had no concept of the universe until just a couple days ago. The only reason I am able to take this all in is because of a new vibration I get from being around these new friends, especially the children".

"With the absence of fear and the vibration of love, our **TRIBE** has opened up to new realities that never existed before yesterday. Our shared experience will never be the same again. We welcome this new experience with excitement".

"New contracts between mice (or all beings) and you hu-manes are being formed. These are silent contracts of knowingness along with trust. Breach of this trust is an act of dis-honor. I speak for myself only but I know the code of honor among mice agrees. We will always act in honor. We forgive you as we forgive ourselves for allowing any past transgressions".

> **When he was finished, you could feel a wave of emotions that reached around the globe. To be forgiven and accepted by mouse-kind formed a new trust agreement for all living things. This was an epic event that was just the beginning of**

many more as the paradoxes of existence were about to unfold in the coming Independence Day celebration.

CHARLES, PENNY and BRANDON all gave demonstrations of their new abilities in a playful skit where PENNY would blow figure bubbles with her sound ability and animate them. CHARLES would give them harder substance so they would not pop when landing and BRANDON gave them speech by throwing his voice into them. They had fairies, dragons, angels, unicorns, birds that flew around the studio. It was a lot of fun. They shared what will always be an example of how we would all play at life, in cooperation with each other, using our abilities to enhance others.

BILL gave an example of just how many perspectives he believes we are completely oblivious to when we look at anything. His new ability was to take in more perspectives. He learned this by not making judgment on anything he views, not putting stops with descriptions or conclusions on anything.

"When we translate anything into words, we are limiting the experience in an attempt to logically understand what one is observing. So free your mind and be ready for new information"!

MARY and MYRA finished by doing a global consciousness reading that promised great results coming from the global sharing. With MARY's assistance MYRA sent out a healing energy to everyone that had any dis-ease. BILL and ALBERT joined in with the sharing.

Myra started out; "welcome everyone to our global healing meditation. There is a wonderful healing that many of you are already familiar with. This meditation has healing powers as well as love intentions".

"Ho'oponopono has been around for many years. Its origin is from Hawaii and we thank those that shared it with the world. We will do our own version of this meditation and we ask that you personalize it as we have".

"Our continued growth as a planet as well as individuals has been full of MIS-TAKES so we are asking for do-overs in this playground of life. First we recognize the natural love we share by saying (**I love you**). Next we recognize that we have make harmful errors and apologize by saying (**I'm sorry**). We then ask (**Please forgive me**) for any offences we have made. Gratitude for our forgiveness is stated as well as appreciation for all of our seemingly un-noticed gifts in life by saying (**Thank you**)".

"I love you, I'm sorry, please forgive me, thank you".

Mary spoke next; "to our wonderful planet Earth that nurtures us as we journey through space and time; **I love you, I'm sorry, please forgive me, thank you".**

Bill; "to all the inhabitants that share this planet with us, be it plant, fish, insect or animal; **I love you, I'm sorry, please forgive me, thank you".**

Albert; "to the elements that make up our world and help us co-create existence; **I love you, I'm sorry, please forgive me, thank you".**

Myra; "to everything that exist alongside us but out of range to our normal sensory perception; **I love you, I'm sorry, please forgive me, thank you".**

Mary; "to the Omni-present; **I love you, I'm sorry, please forgive me, thank you".**

Bill; "to the unimaginable vastness of infinity; **I love you, I'm sorry, please forgive me, thank you".**

Albert; "to our own vessel that we reside in, that is riding along on this journey through experience, our connection within to creation; **I love you, I'm sorry, please forgive me, thank you".**

After the broadcast on the World Network, the group went right back to the research lab.

Mary suggested; "since we have always journeyed into the past, let us make a journey into the future to see the results of the Gateway's Global Sharing. I know we can only witness probabilities but it will help in analyzing the best presentation". "How do you like that idea"?

Everyone agreed; "yes, let's do it".

> **They all began immediately preparing for their next vision journey. They also agreed to only go one year into the future because they realized that there would be many variables to the future, depending on just what takes place. This would help them determine any preparation they may need to implement.**

> "Everything we think and do in *the here and now has effect on where we are tomorrow*", Mary remarked.

> *"This is just a way of insuring* the best possible results".

The journey began with the gateway spinning counterclockwise. The next stop was THE UNIVERSE.

ZEB appeared immediately, *"welcome back, my Friends. Please understand that your thoughts about keeping close to the current event is very important, because the further you go into the future the more alternative realities there will be. I suggest you only look at the most probable timelines given the recent experiences".*

In an instant, the group was looking at what seemed like the same world they had just left, although they also felt many subtle changes. ALBERT noticed that his father was with them and MARY's Aunt Jill, who had both passed away just recently. So ALBERT thought they had gone off course into a previous timeline where they hadn't passed away.

Zeb assured him; *"that this was indeed the father Albert once knew and that here, in this timeline, you have found a way to bring him back with you.* **MARY**'s *Aunt Jill also chose to come back to the physical reality to finish her needed evolution and learn the missing lessons she needed. She was grateful for the chance to operate in a reality that was supportive of her spiritual growth and keep the learned knowledge up to her untimely demise. Even your departed souls are being given the opportunity to finish their ascension in this lifetime. They can choose to return or be reborn into another life, if they have not completed their journey to the higher dimensions".*

"Mankind is being given every opportunity or advantage they can get to finish their awakening and joining with the creators source. Some have chosen to come back to help others. Some came back just to experience the blossoming of mankind into the age of enlightenment, to partake in the wonderful physical Three Dimensional realm that was now transforming to heaven on earth. Out of the billions of possible realities that are possible, they chose to return to this one".

As they moved forward all could feel a vibration in the field that was not part of their familiar senses. It was like the unconditional love vibration was reaching new levels of harmony creating a soothing frequency that brought instant contentment. The group noticed a lot of the technical tools that they felt so attached to were no longer around. Spiritual growth had out sourced the need for technology. Why should you build a spaceship when you can travel across the cosmos with a thought? Why have cell phones when we can project and communicate telepathically, with anyone, anywhere?

The playful, genius inhabitants of this timeline have taken co-creators to a new meaning. Where the driving force is improving creation and bringing value to existence for everyone.

With all the future individuals have learned they are still thirsty for new knowledge and further comprehension. They

> find happiness in the path of learning that never ends. They find humor in knowing nothing after learning so much.
>
> The inter-galactic community that some consider the subconscious of the universe is no longer concerned about mankind's destructive or self-destructive ways, as they have passed that threshold on the path to source.

Some mayor change had taken place that Mary was keenly aware of. "I'm picking up on the soothing harmony that permeated this time stream. I'm not picking up any mental chatter from anyone's mind. It is as if we, as a species, had shut down that inner dialog that our left brain uses to define existence, limiting reality to the five outer senses. If more and more people are using their heart-mind then this learned chatter would stop. Like the mind of a child, our ability to learn will increase in a phenomenal way".

"Before we leave this time line", Zeb asked; "I would like you all to witness one more event".

> With that, they all went off planet to a large galactic gathering of beings representing almost all life forms in the universe. The cathedral was built like a vortex. In the center of the vortex was a being speaking to all the beings.
>
> The voice could be heard in every dialect possible because no actual words were being spoken, it was more like a consciousness projection.

INTERGALATIC BEING

"Representatives of the oneness, there is a birth taking place on a tiny planet within the Milky Way Galaxy in the Solar System called Sol on the planet Earth. Many of you may have felt the energy coming from this region for some time now and know that they are becoming constructive, conscious co-creators of existence. We are here now to officially welcome this marvelous speck and its indigenous species into the cosmic fold of prime creation.

Many out there choose to visit this gem to help it along knowing the potential that they could achieve. Even the representative that sent emissaries there with destructive intent only succeeded in teaching these earthlings the values they now bring to all on Earth as well as the cosmos".

"Make this a time of contemplative celebration by taking the new energy coming from this marvel and returning to it in kind. Welcome this new species that joins us in balancing the universe. Everything is right on schedule within the divine creator".

ALBERT was noticing all the surrounding architecture. This architecture looks very much like the structures I saw in Ancient Lemuria. Could this be the garden city that planted seeds on Earth thousands of years ago?

ZEB returned everyone to Earth in a blink.

"As you can see what is happening on your Earth has far reaching affects that we can only begin to guess. I am just a student of the universe myself".

Mary noted; *"we have come so far in just one year, and we should visit other possibilities before ending our journey".*

> **Instantly, with that thought, they were in another timeline and this one was also very subtle in differences. The first thing they noticed was the absence of their lost friends and relatives.**
>
> **They witnessed ALBERT, in his future form, asking verbally for MARY to link minds with him. He was aware that they would be on this journey and was risking communication even though it may cause a paradox.**

ZEB advised against a mind link. "**ALBERT**, *she is already linked to you now. Your future ALBERT seemed to know this, so listen".*

ALBERT's alternative future being

The missing ingredient to a successful Independence Day is the intent of the individual making up the world consciousness. Love must be the driving intent or you will fall short of what can be accomplished. Here, there is still a great division among the population. Many who ascended have chosen not to hang around because those without the light have used their new knowledge to create minions of followers working towards their own selfish gain. Some of mankind has taken a step backwards on the evolutionary ladder pulling others down with them. They have distorted the gift given to them. All is not wrong, however, I was with you on the journey you are on now and I have no recollection of any warning being given, so I am only hoping you happen to choose this timeline. My abilities have worn off and someone has hidden the Gateway away from humanity.

You have one and one-half days to raise the love vibration of humanity to fully reach the desired pathway. The pathway that I witnessed on our journey last year is not how it turned out.

With that said, the group was whisked away to the final timeline before their return. In this reality they saw technology still developing and the dependence on it still prevalent to man's existence. Many strides have been made, even on a cosmic spiritual level, only the logical left brain has still limited the development into the higher planes of existence. New thresholds were being overcome daily, even though it was a slower progression towards the true potential man could reach. The Gateway seemed to be missing in this reality also. Is this man's greatest chance for mass ascension?

Next they were all back in the lab, aware of their best course of action. The thought energies experienced by everyone was shared.

MARY now links all the thoughts of the travelers to review the vision journey.

"The higher our love vibration, the further we will progress. This made sense to them all along only now it became of paramount importance. We must all tap into our heart centers to make this journey the key to leaping up the evolutionary ladder to levels we are all capable of doing. The Gateway is just a stepping stone while the real change takes place within each individual. Only by tapping into our source or connection to the universe can we hope to achieve true wisdom".

Albert thoughts; "since I see all of you nodding in agreement with what Mary just shared, then the best way to spread the word is by sharing the experience in another global broadcast. Inspiration is always the key to learning, so we need to inspire the love vibration with examples. We must broadcast it ourselves for it to be felt by everyone else".

Myra's thoughts; "we would not even need the Gateway if we can get most of us to tap into our heart centers. We have a great task ahead of us and I believe this is the best group to accomplish this".

With this said they all went their separate way. BILL hung around to inform the essence workers of the task ahead. *USE* **was a type of company that helped people play at work within the passion they hold in life. This allowed for the creative instinct to be encouraged and developed. As a result they had one of the best teams in the world working on this project.**

Each person worked within their expertise with others that may have varying degrees of experience that mostly share without ego, knowing it was for the greater good of our evolution. This was truly the company to spread the love vibration because it flowed here so freely. They all played at their work and accomplished more than before imagined.

Action was taken by everyone with an excitement that had its own chord and shared the same vibration. Meditations

were planned, dancing was encouraged; this was like all the joys of the holidays without a bit of greed or malice. Only gratefulness, benevolence, love, compassion, laughter, contentment and opening your heart were spread like a wave that encompassed the globe.

People welcomed this feeling with awe. They knew that this was their natural state. That they could achieve, see and feel everyone around them. It is remarkable, as each one reaches this same awareness, even the planet responded to this wealth of love vibration.

Time was almost meaningless as the planet was changing every few moments instead of every so many weeks, month or years. Reaching into your heart center, where everything just IS, was the only way to keep up with the changes. A new era was birthing!

Wave after wave of change occurred that could one could ride out or get overcome by. No one was left to drown as everyone was reaching out to help each other. Some would reject the changes, holding on to past psychopathic behaviors that were soon to become obsolete. This old behavior would only be a reminder of who we chose not to be.

CHAPTER 9

POWER PLAY

There were still a few individuals left in the world that saw the Gateway as a way to re-gain control of the masses. They began a smear campaign telling everyone that the Gateway was a mind control devise and it was their duty to save the planet by removing this great threat.

By having the Gateway all to themselves, they would create an unfair advantage over everyone. Everything was moving very fast, so they did not waste any time with their plans to stop the world tour and take the Gateway for their own use. The remaining cabal glory seekers met in a secure location to plan the heist and also discuss previous attempts at global dominance. They had many new obstacles to overcome because the people were not easily manipulated anymore. Code name were given to all that attended. MISS DIS-INFORMATION (ex-CIA operative and liaison with FBI), PHARMACEUTICAL PHYLLIS (attorney for the FDA), ORLIE ILLUSIONIST (publicist for the president in 2011), FIAT FEDRALIA (former head of St Louis Federal Reserve), RESOURCE RAPER (was former Under Secretary of the UN), MILITARY MONGREL (secret operative in the Pentagon),

AGRICULTURAL AGGRESSOR (head of the Agriculture Bureau) and FIAT FRANK (money slave driver) all attended. It is hard to imagine that this primitive thinking still existed but as weak as the cabal had become they still had illusionary dreams of supreme domination with a subject class society serving them.

MISS DIS-INFORMATION; "I remember our old tactics of fear, labeling, miss-information, creating statistics, the divide to conquer and mistrust are not as effective as they once used to be. Therefore, it is important that **we** the present day cabal are aware that we may have one more attempt to gain world dominion. We will have to put all of our cards out for this last ditch attempt for our return to power. As long as the people continue thinking with their heart-mind, where real truth is found, none of those old tricks would work. Time is not on our side, we must move quickly to get the Gateway from the world".

PHARMACEUTICAL PHYLLIS; "our dark forces in the old days operated by convincing the ignorant populace that our forces were the higher authority, whether it was the government, religion, media, scholars or corporations. The truth was all were corporations ruled from behind the scene with profit as their only goal. We sure had the best driving force on profit and control, which did not survive the shift mankind took from thinking with the brain to thinking with the heart. Those old ideals of ours only brought pain and destruction to the overall good of the planet, which those masses didn't like. It's a shame the cabal plan no longer served the old global consciousness. Even dumbing the people down using prescription drugs along with GMO foods did not work".

ORLIE ILLUSIONIST; "the wise use of natural resources along with mankind's return to naturalism versus materialism out-sourced the glutinous old paradigm, 'sure messed with our plans'. That new technology (meant for us only) soared to new levels, as cooperation of learned experiences and experiments were shared for the common good. Who were those unseen helpers that changed the masses way of thinking? I never understood that time period".

FIAT FEDRALIA; "when the dark forces lost control of the financial system, in a maneuver to gain even more control, we were very surprised to see that no-one was looking to us for answers anymore. Instead the masses were acting together, can you imagine that, to bring about better solutions that would benefit the majority of the population. These new ideals just leveled out the playing field for everyone, where value offered were not illusionary. It sure took the steam out of our engines at that time".

RESOURCE RAPER; "I really got upset when people were remembering who they really are in their connection to each other and connection to the Source, which was the real turning point for the world. Money, as a slave master, was not accepted anymore".

"Remember that obscene slogan: 'If we have to serve a master, it should be our own Source connection in our heart center,' shouted the populace". "If one is truly operating from this higher, more harmonious place, then we would never bring harm to anything." "That really made me sick".

"Also the beginning of the end started with acceptance with detachment as a role in the great shift of 2011 through 2015. People stopped fighting the system and just detached themselves from that albatross. Creating something new and better became the focus. I really lost it then. It is time for our come back and it has to be NOW".

MILITARY MONGREL; "if our old system wants to start a war somewhere, we no longer has the support of these people. These people are too busy creating a better life to bother about anyone's bid for control over others or control over resources; because the masses finally understand that nothing could happen without their energy, which they no longer gave out freely. Without the people's energy, we faded into history and that era ended, when we review it, you can see it as a blind period in our evolution".

AGRICULTURAL AGGRESSOR; "our vain attempts at causing fear by our small persistent groups of value destroyers makes little difference in these people's lives. So taking the Gateway must become our top priority. We know we cannot steal it while it was in the *USE* building, so our master plans and contingency plans must be made to snatch the Gateway while it is on that world tour".

FIAT FRANK; "there are still groups out there that believe they still need to make all of their exchanges using something with common values as an exchange medium, like money. However, these new energies show that most trade now are evenly distributed among the populace without the taxable exchange instrument that gave the old populace no real value. That is why our group of people must work smarter to steal the Gateway. Money used to be our control tool, which was what we used to sell mankind into slavery. We created the money so that made us the masters. We want that power back. Our form of slavery was abolished and the world went through some troubling times before these insane people worked it out themselves without government or corporate intervention. Can you believe that? Without our help or ruling"! "Disgusting"!

MISS DIS-INFORMATION; "their value production and resources became their main means of exchange. Weights and measures were re-evaluated. Even physical labor was all mechanized. People really did not have to work at all. Then those people naturally, get that term, "naturally" started developing within themselves the passions that made them the happiest. Happiness is for animals that wage their tails. Did you get that creations the individuals did brought value as a form of play rather than the old drudgery of full time slave job. Do you remember when they started making human life and planet Earth as the highest priority in almost everyone's life? Even those that were physically challenged became more resourceful than they ever were by overcoming their handicaps and contributing in ways that enriched humanity in multiple ways. I lost so many slaves and societal leches to that crazy idea".

PHARMACEUTICAL PHYLLIS; "what got me was that this mankind idea was improving on biological longevity each day as now the possibility of the average lifespan has become two hundred fifty years. That **MYRA** person has a passion to help cure man's biggest disease, death. Don't they get it? Death is best when we can monetize it".

AGRICULTURAL AGGRESSOR; "alright, group, let's get to work together again. The world's wealth is our incentive to each other. Therefore, let's successfully steal the Gateway. For it is power beyond belief. Then we destroy the Gateway forever. We can give the other groups what they would use for themselves and break any pre-arrangement with them. That is the nature of how our great self-centered, primitive crabs of humanity survived. This new way the people think and act that made them think we were the piranhas. We will look at all the stopping points of the tour and make our plans work accordingly to snatch the Gateway. Let's get going".

MILITARY MONGREL; "there is full closure from *USE* about the tour and all of its stopping points so this gives us a great advantage. This sure is a weakness or stupidity of these organizers. It sure helps us. After all, nobody at *USE* knows our plans or whereabouts".

ALL 8 CABAL LEADERS IN UNISON; *"this surprise will give us the advantage we need"*. **Insane laugher rings out rumbling across the dark world of the cabal. "Bwaa-ha-haaaa"!**

> **Meanwhile, the feel good sharing taking place around the planet was spreading like a ripple across a still pond. This wave, if recorded on a planetary grid, would resemble a sun shower on this same still pond with each droplet of rain causing ripples that overlap each other as they vibrated outward. Depending on one's perspective, for some the waves were tsunamis.**
>
> **You can feel the Hawaiian vibration spread.**
>
> **Dancing was contagious as large groups let the inner music take them where they felt the happiest. People danced alone. They danced together. They danced with the universe. They**

opened their arms and embraced the seven directions. They stretched their arms out to the North and all that existed by unity consciousness. The people, the vegetation, the mountains, the fauna, the source within everything, joined the energy that danced all the way around the globe in each direction. Bringing their arms back in with the affection of finding a lost lover, everyone took it all into their heart center with a whisper of unconditional love.

Asian vibration

People reached out to the East, the South and then the West embracing all that existed in those directions. Then they reached up, reached out to embrace the upper cosmos. Next they reached down below to Mother Earth that cared for them so deeply and asked for forgiveness as they embraced her home. From here they opened their arms to welcome everything that was the internal universe that existed within every cell, atom and molecule of our body. Everyone's thoughts, emotions, habits, conscious or un-conscious thoughts, dreams and desires were embraced with a whisper in all the directions with unconditional love.

European vibration

This dancing became a smash success everywhere. Large groups were getting together to perform in public places. It was a spectacular sight to behold with the energy that it created being pleasantly infective. Songs were written overnight that had music accompanying the lyrics that held those frequencies that brought good feelings to everyone.

This loving energy reached out and permeated throughout all existence further than anyone could imagine. A global atmosphere of united conscious love for each other had never been reached until this time as another world changing event took place.

Albert was amazed at how everyone shared freely. "It is wonderful all that we are hearing that is happening around the world. Surely nothing could stop this global ascension from taking place. As individuals, we co-create the micro universe as well as the macro universe in ways we are not even aware of, until, as a collective consciousness, the harmonics are without limits that cannot be described in words. How marvelous that feels. It vibrates through my being".

Scout; "this coming new dark, you call night, before Independence Day, reminds us to return to our **TRIBE**. We have so much to share about these wonderful or magical stories we just finished".

Returning to the tribe, Scout gives them his version of the events that took place. The hu-manes, using just their spirits, took us a trip to places that only existed as if the events had taken place in another time. You could create and better your own lives by doing something different about what you are doing today".

"How will that help our TRIBE", Babbler asks? "How can we improve lives of all the mice in the world? Can we do something while you are on the tour?"

"Great questions and ideas, **BABBLER**, let us make a plan," Scout felt excitement about this idea. "We can split up our **TRIBE** going on the tour so each **TRIBE** mouse could, along the tour route, gather mice from all over the planet bringing them to the Gateway. So the evolutionary changes would enhance the new mice just like this **TRIBE** shares now".

Wisdom mouse speaks humbly; "this will bring a new age to mice-kind everywhere. We may even learn from our new friends. We can teach them the mistakes to avoid that created a lot of harmful behavior in our development as a current enlightened species. Our tribe has been developing for many generations so what we have to share will help others avoid many miss-takes".

Scout spoke up again; "the hu-manes had been destructive to themselves and everything around them for such a long time. They

107

even committed genocide on a lot of species that shared the world with them. Hu-manes used us for experiments or amusement as they thought we were the inferior species. That has changed for the most part now. We are rising to a new level of existence. It will take our community planning and action to bring it to reality".

The excitement grew amid the TRIBE even though many did not fully understand what was going on. They felt the energy! Then Squeamish started tapping his fingers on a metal duct that had a catchy beat to it. Cracker whistled along with the beat, while Jasmine started moving her hips to the beat, Scout grabbed her hand and started dancing with her.

Cheezer started scratching on a rippled section of metal that made the sound of a washboard, that's when things got really lively. They all had that feel good feeling.

Dazzler starts singing with a playful voice;

> Grab a partner and swing them around.
> then help them up off the ground,
> Move together to and fro,
> then step forward and away you go.
> Wave your arms in the air
> then move around without a care.
>
> Yee-ha, hoo-ha, let's have some fun;
> because our journey has just begun.
>
> Step up now and do a dip,
> those that can, will do a flip.
> Tie your tails on a knot
> then all grab hands and begin to trot.
> Take some time to have some fun
> for tomorrow we will be on the run.

Free, free, free at last,
all of our worries in the past'
The time is ripe for us to see,
on this fact we all agree,
For what our scout had to say,
will bring about a better day.

Yee-ha, hoo-ha, let's have some fun;
because our journey has just begun.

As our ties with past are shaken,
it is time for us to awaken.
Our goal is now crystal clear,
our destiny we should not fear.
So dance tonight while we can,
for tomorrow we begin our plan.

Yee-ha, hoo-ha, let's have some fun;
because our journey has just begun.

The free spirit of the mice continued all night. The TRIBE only got a couple hours sleep before they had to meet with ALBERT and the GROUP.

The pre-event meeting started right on schedule. MYRA attended as a holographic image on the holo-phone. Teams were chosen and, much to ALBERT's surprise, the mice decided to split up into teams as well.

Bill announces; "here is the roster for the teams: **ALBERT, CHARLES** and **MARY** are teamed up with **CHEEZER, CRACKER** and **BENN**.

BRANDON, MYRA and **I** will be teamed up with **SQUEAMISH, BELCHER, DAZZLER** and **RUNNER**. **PENNY** and **ADRIAN** will have **SCOUT, JASMINE** and **BABBLER**". "Did I leave anyone out that signed up to go with us"?

Adrian chimes in: "we leave in five hours. The first three stops will be the Philippines briefly, with the event in Japan, **MALAYSIA** and Australia. We will arrive to these locations at 12:01 a.m. as their day is just beginning. The bullet trains leave at 10:30 this evening with the trip taking only one and half-hours".

Albert explains; "there is an 8 hour time difference between here and there, so you will have time to rest before the events start. I do not have time to explain linear time to the mice, so all I can say is make sure you stay with your group at all cost. In order for this to go smoothly, we must all be ready to move when each event is over".

"Our teams of inventors have put together some communication devices, along with clothing and other gadgets, you will find useful to get around these new areas".

Looking through the gifts Albert brought, Scout asks; "are these little bags filled with the communication things"? "How do we use them"?

Assuring Scout and the mice, Albert tells them; "I know you will find uses for these things. Our creative team has been working on these things since we met you. The clothing is like ours in that it forms to fit your physique and also has properties to keep you comfortable in all kinds of weather. We have tracking devices for these events only. Usually it is only by free choice that these devices are used. Remember, we do not want to mis-place anyone so we will use them in this occasion. I will carry this device because it will track your location and your health statistics. This will let us know that no one is hurt or injured while we are travelling at such a rapid pace".

Mary adds; "**TRIBE,** check this image of the planet in this three dimensional hologram with 3 different colors circling the globe. You can see these are the paths each team is taking on the tour. Each stop is marked with a circle".

Addressing his tribe, Scout tells them; "**TRIBE**, I know we have never seen so much wonder, so ask the questions, you are afraid to ask".

BABBLER is bursting with questions. "You mean we all live on that ball all together? We lived in the same house with each other before, now we all share this home? How come it took so long for us to start getting along"?

Everyone laughed

Scout; "these plans are so involved with the imagery, so dazzling, we will have to review them".

> **Scout forgot to tell Albert or anyone, for that matter, the TRIBE's plans to help mice around the world evolve along with mankind. With only 3 hours to departure time, the travelers all retreated to make their personal preparations. They would meet at the train station an hour before blast off.**

The TRIBE gathered to wish the travelers farewell. Dressed in their new clothing and equipped with gadgets they had yet to figure out how to use; Scout with his brave explorers waved to all remaining behind.

CHAPTER 10

THE TOUR BEGINS

The teams gathered at the James Hill Bullet Train Dock to take off on the world tour with the Gateway. They were surrounded by hundreds of people that came to see them take off on their history making journey. Cameras were flashing. The media was asking questions to all the team members.

With all the excitement, Scout calmed his friends. "**TRIBE,** we have never experienced anything like this. Let us realize that this is just a preview of things to come within the next portion of our lives. You all look great dressed up in full gear. These Hu-manes have never seen a display of our species exhibited like this".

The children were putting on a show for the cameras and crowd. Penny organizes the playground; "I will make blowing shape bubbles of birds, fairies, dragons, elves, and anything I can imagine. **CHARLES,** give them solidity, please. I just love doing this with you, **CHARLES,** and seeing all this love. This is incredible fun for all of the people in the playground at the train station. What a way to start our journeys".

The time had now come for them to enter the vehicles to head towards their destinations. These brave messengers all embraced or did their own unique way of expressing affection before they entered their separate vehicles.

Before boarding Albert talks to the teams. "Your mother and I have complete confidence in you, children. Your new little friends are as precious to us as you are. Love to you all. Hug up now".

As each group entered their train cabin vehicles, they were fascinated by these dining cars which offered an array of entertainment as well as places for rest and solitude. There was even a garden area. In addition, the whole trip was being recorded in holographic images for placement in the archives within the world computer library.

The train cars pulled in and mechanical arms lifted the vehicles to be placed snugly into place. Each car of the train was linked and could become detachable at any time. They would all travel as a linked convoy. At certain junctions, the cars would split to go to their different destinations.

Task programmed robots were around to handle all of the adventurers needs on the journey. The vehicles were domed in Plexiglas for a panoramic view of all the surroundings, even though they were moving so fast that it looked like a streak. The rail beds of the train had cameras placed strategically to provide a slower version of what was outside and displayed on monitors on the lower panes of the cars.

Albert pondered thoughtfully; "**MARY,** just what did it take to accomplish this fantastic link around the world? I remember when things like this were only thought of in science fiction books. What of all the essences, talents, collaboration and cooperation that it took to make this train a reality. Surveyors, tectonics plate specialist, engineers, designers, manufacturers, scientist, inventors, workers and technicians as the list continue on and on".

"Man could never have accomplished this in a fiat monetary based economy. In a resource/value based economy with people working together it seemed like nothing was impossible. We are in a universe of abundance that is no longer controlled by the few and no longer fueled by greed or power".

"**ALBERT**, darling, I am so proud of what has been accomplished, I know you share this feeling with millions of others who played a part in bringing the world society and all of these wonders to success. Your gratefulness is shining as you ponder the past. We are now playing a new role in bringing about creation and change that you do so well. **CHARLES** is asking for you, he wants to play rehearsal and he is very excited".

> **As the cars detached to go off to different destinations you could not even feel a thing. The transition was so smooth it did not slow them down at all. Albert and Charles watched on the monitors as they went in the desired directions and said good-bye to the others on their communicators.**
>
> **In the other car, PENNY and the others had to smile as BABBLER would not shut up during the first part of the trip. He saw wonder in everything followed up with questions.**

Babbler rambling: "look at all the humans, just how many are there? Hey look, it's us on that moving picture. Hey, it's repeating me and everything I do. What's up with that? Hey, **SCOUT**, check this out, that human child is wearing your face. Does he think that he is you? These beings are funny. Why did we fear each other"?

With a smile, Penny tells Babbler; "listening to you, **BABBLER,** is like listening to a talk show radio host that loved to hear his own voice. Take it all in, my friend, only you can find the answers to all of your questions. What we tell you is just our perspective".

> **Babbler would remain quiet for a while then you could see the same excitement, perplexity, and chatter going on even in his silent mode. Instead of talking, he just made quiet noises.**

Unable to contain himself, BABBLER finally blurts out; "*oh, huh, auhh, ha, hummm!*. Where are all the others of our kind"?

Meanwhile ADRIAN is talking into her communicator to her staff; "yes, we are on schedule. There are still a number of actions to do to orchestrate the events ahead of us. You would get such a kick out of **BABBLER** and all the others at the love and intent that everyone felt for everyone". "Oh, do not go too far away from us, **BABBLER**".

In the last car with BILL, MYRA and their team, BILL is busy studying the monitors that displayed the surroundings along the route of the journey.

"**MYRA,** although were traveling at an alarming rate, I can use my photographic memory to take in every scene. This data stream recording and the technology within my headset sees and hears the entire different spectrums as well as the vibrations that are available. I could make this trip several times and still not get enough learning".

MYRA is busy interacting with the biological science foundation on the holo-phone. "**BILL**, I hear you only I'm attending a conference geared towards biological longevity. We are so close to some major breakthroughs that even the excitement of this journey could not stop me from this research. I know for certain what I will learn on this journey feels like a major puzzle piece for the goal our Foundation is achieving".

> **SQUEAMISH, BELCHER and RUNNER played together while going through their back packs.**

Belcher swung his hook around throwing it as it gained momentum. "Look where my grappler hook landed on the table. Tie the other end to one of the monitors across the room so we can practice walking across the string to get to places we could not reach under normal conditions".

Runner ran up the string; "I got the lead, I'm the champion. C'mon guys, follow me".

> RUNNER stood in triumph at the top encouraging the others to follow. The mice explored the whole vehicle using the tools that the humans had provided. This practice would definitely help them find other mice while on their journey as well as cause problems keeping the team together.

MALAYSIA: The first stop on the sojourn would prove to be the most challenging. Malaysia was full of other mice that would play a big role in the evolution on this trip. This group of travelers would learn more about the nature of human development than they could ever have imagined as the Gateway guided them through the conscious and sub-consciousness of the species called hu-manes, as the TRIBE of mice laughingly called them. With each Gateway activation, it would bring the mice closer to understanding mankind.

The train arrived in Borneo and the mice had a spider web of string all over the car stretching in every direction as BILL and MYRA laughingly worked their way out through whatever exit that appeared easiest. BELCHER was right behind RUNNER with SQUEAMISH riding in the top pocket of BILL's uniform. The mice had little time to rest as preparations were made for the show ahead.

Belcher was the first to remind the other of their side quest. "C'mon, resting is not part of our plan, we have a side motive to attend to and that is the gathering of the local mice. Quiet, we'll wait until **BILL, BRANDON** and **MYRA** are sleeping, then we take off. **SQUEAMISH**, you're in charge of watching the hu-manes".

> The mice took their gear and went out on the streets of Borneo. At the rear of the first Café they came to, RUNNER

saw others of his kind; he was feeling their fear of him in the outfit he was wearing and that he walked upright on two legs. The city mice ran away.

Runner; "*This was going to be harder than we thought*".

One brave mouse approached them. RUNNER AND BELCHER were being circled by a Borneo mouse called Bravo in the alley.

Bravo was very intimidating; "I do not know whether to laugh or cry. You look so ridiculous, yet what you represent is so despicable. Why would you act and dress like the Mongol race of hu-manes"?

Scared BELCHER burped a large gut belch; "Arrrppp, Laugh, burpppp"! "You may be more like us than I thought", Bravo snickers.

The other mice came out from hiding at the sound of friendly laughter, while being cautious as they approached. Belcher burped uncontrollably.

Runner replied; "my friend speaks for both of us".

This simple play of levity lightened the mood for the other mice as they came even closer to check out the two strange critters that looked like them but dressed like hu-manes.

BELCHER rips out a series of belches. "We arpp here(arppp) to helppppp"!

Even Runner was laughing now.

Bravo snapped; "so you think we need help? How could you, traitors, help us? Look at you"!!

The tension returned to RUNNER's demeanor as certain strength also filled his spirit. Getting down on all four legs, he walked closer to the gathering crowd. Just then, one of the Café workers came

through the doors into the alley. Seeing all the mice, he picked up a broom and scattered them.

RUNNER and BELCHER grabbed their string tying it to whatever was around and crossing the angry worker's path. The string, being too hard to spot, caused the worker to trip, ending up grinding the ground with his face, which caused the rest of the mice to cheer for the new arrivals.

In a safe and secluded location, they welcomed their new heroes.

Runner explained to the other mice; "there is a new awareness which is about to change the course of history for this whole planet. Brothers and Sisters, do you know just how big the world is? Communication with each of us is slow because only a few of you understand the concepts that I'm telling all of you. I have learned this in only 4 dark nights and 5 light days. I did not know anything in comparison to what I have learned".

"Be sure to be under the stage of the largest building you know where hu-manes gather in mass, just in the middle of darkness. You will be a part of the greatest experience you have ever had in your life. Spread the word around town in the mean time to get more of our species to the event".

Now comfortable with Belcher and Runner, Bravo tells them; "this spot is well known to us, as we have a feast when the humans gather there. Droppings are everywhere; we will go there for the feast alone. Yummie...."

With this the MICE all took off running along the rafters, walls, crevices, through holes only a mouse could get through. SQUEAMISH's voice came out of RUNNER's communicator in his pocket.

"The hu-manes are looking all over for you. You have to return, hurry"!!

One of the stragglers in the stampede heard the radio, squeaked. "He speaks out of his chest in a different voice"!

Concerned Runner asks; "**BELCHER**, do you know how to get back to the team"?

"No (burp)"

Runner answers; "**SQUEAMISH**, we'll meet you all at the auditorium, if we can find it. Our new friends think they know where it is. I hope it is the right place. Hurry, **BELCHER**, let's follow our new friends".

Through holes in walls then down gutters and wires they ran. In storm sewers, they gathered more of their kind as the group expanded into the hundreds, even thousands all heading in the same direction, towards the arena. Most of them had no idea where and why they were following. This innocence would prove to be very confusing when they have their first realization ever. For now they were heading towards a possible feast.

Mid-dark was very soon with the race on. RUNNER held BELCHER's hand so they would not be parted during the mad race. BELCHER had a hard time keeping up so they had to stop on several occasions. Many of the regular mice gave them strange glances seeing those two wearing hu-mane cloths; however, the thought of food overwhelmed their curiosity.

Lurking behind a nearby trash can, watching the gathering of mice increase was Purr-puss the cat. This feast of mice could not be ignored. Stalking the herd would be fruitful from a higher vantage so Purr-puss worked his way up a nearby stairwell crouching down to plunge on his desired prey. The stragglers in the herd would be an easy dinner.

Runner had stopped to allow Belcher to gulp some air as Purr-puss leaped on some mice nearby. Runner pulled his

string out while heading towards the fray. Runner jumped on Purr-puss' back and rode him like a bronco. Purr-puss went crazy with his dinner on his back; he lunged at the other mice while Runner pulled his head back. Runner managed to get his string into Purr-puss' mouth and pulled back with all his muscles.

A crowd of mice spectators gathered to witness this act of bravery that they had never seen before. Fleeing was always the first choice or instinct for the mice, so Runner's actions were spectacular. Belcher got hold of Purr-puss' tail and was being thrown about like a child's toy; the belching was coming from both ends but Belcher also hung on. Some of the braver mice leaped on Purr-puss as he started to become tired and they persevered as Purr-puss fell over from exhaustion.

Meanwhile Runner was still on Purr-puss' back; he scratched Purr-puss' neck in a friendly soothing way as he spoke directly into the cat's ear in a confident whisper.

"Your days of chasing us are over. A new contact between us that is equal and beneficial for us both species is now in place".

Purr-puss responded to the new energy that he was feeling even though he did not fully comprehend what Runner was saying. The head scratching felt kind of good! Belcher had worked his way to sit behind Runner as Purr-puss rose to his feet; he now had two passengers guiding his direction.

"Take us to the Gateway, follow the crowd. Let's move". "You (urp) heard (gulp) the (achh) mouse! **Go**"!

Off they went towards the arena. The other mice scattered out of Purr-puss' way and cheered as they noticed the passengers he was carrying. Runner and Belcher held on tight as the arena came into view. Dodging the gathering people they made it into the arena unnoticed by most.

CHAPTER 11

GROUP CONSCIOUSNESS

The bullet train arrives in Australia with PENNY, ADRIAN, SCOUT, JASMINE and BABBLER

After getting only a short rest before going to the stadium, the team left the train. People from all over the country were waiting for their arrival. They were greeted by Dan Freeman who ushered them to the back stage to prepare for the event.

Dan greets the team assuring them; "the Gateway has arrived and there would be fifteen minutes wait before activation. That will give you enough time for introductions, OK? Cameras are set up at different locations and a large screen monitor is hung above the stage. Timing is critical to allow for the teleporter too send the Gateway to the next location for another team. Adrian will make the introductions".

The team enters the stage as the crowd gives them a standing ovation. The lights on the stage danced around them in a kaleidoscope of colors. Adrian steps up to the podium.

Adrian; "it gives me great honor to introduce this exhilarating team, one of three such teams circling the world. I realize you are as excited as I am, so we will be quick in our introductions. **PENNY** is the second child of Albert and Mary Jennings. These youngsters each have gained tremendous skills".

"**PENNY,** show us the beautiful bubble fantasy figures through your soap wand".

> **Penny produced an array of figures that marveled everyone. The crowd roared with applause as SCOUT, JASMINE and BABBLER stepped on stage. SCOUT waved his arms to quiet everyone.**
>
> **The Gateway was lowered onto the stage as the lights dimmed in the stadium.**

Babbler spoke without rambling; "everyone, please take several refreshing breaths and clear your minds as **SCOUT** starts the Gateway spinning".

> **A soothing vibration filled the stadium and calm was immediately felt within everyone. The evolution of the universe appeared as a Three Dimensional image that engulfed the entire stadium. Consciousness was felt deep within each person as they witnessed The Big Bang. Within seconds, galaxies started to form as the Universe took shape. Collisions of matter appeared violent, however, as each collision occurred new creations formed that had never before existed.**
>
> **Moments later as everything took shape, the crowd witnessed that the collisions continued in a much more subtle way. They began to realize that collisions were a never ending creative process that brought new things into existence. Each instant passed; continually formed into the reality of the next moment.**

They watched as the Milky Way galaxy took shape. The scene focused in on Sol, the solar system. Billions of light years flashed by as the scene continued to now focus on just the planet Earth. Violent collisions continued as the Earth got bombarded by meteors from the galaxy, bringing with them the basic building blocks for life. The cosmic stage was set for consciousness to evolve as the Earth became a water world.

Microscopic organisms started to take shape as the collisions continued. As an increased rate that seemed to now develop survival in ways that insured the progression of life in a conscious way. Each challenge brought about a new form that was able to survive by adapting to the challenges the universe brought forth.

Land was formed and the water creatures found their way up on the land to a whole new set of challenges and development. It was as if life was a receiver of universal data being broadcast to this new plain of awareness. Death brought new life, like the changes of the seasons. Each new life form had adapted to the challenges confronting them. Mass extinctions took place, as life continued to develop, with new ways of coping with the surrounding environments. Each new life seemed to pass on a small memory of the previous life and left some evidence behind of its former existence.

Everyone in the stadium could feel their connection with all of these previous development stages of life, as if they had lived them. They all felt that they were a part of this cosmic scene that has brought them to where they are today in the stadium.

The audience watched as the tectonic plates shifted on this planet and the land got separated from one large land mass, the continent of Pangaea, into two smaller land masses, that we are familiar with today. Ice ages came and went, as the

Earth developed further. The history of man went by in the blink of an eye. Everyone felt the changes as man went through its evolution with a rush of enlightenment.

All of this was shared by the whole stadium and was broadcast around the world for all to experience. Mankind would never be the same because of this infusion of knowledge into their minds as each experience from the Gateway brought about a different awareness.

The lights in the stadium came on as the Gateway slowed to a stop. The crowd, sitting motionless, was left in awe with a feeling of extreme comfort and love. The changes brought about within each individual remained to be seen as each person had never before felt empowered like this.

A new sense of purpose arose in our team of travelers as the Gateway was teleported to the next location.

Penny hurried the team; "C'mon, team let's head to the bullet train to go to our next location".

Meanwhile, ALBERT, MARY, CHARLES, CHEEZER, CRACKER and BENN were entering the stage in an auditorium in Japan.

They met with Anna Baby Love and family in the Philippines before moving the enlarged team to Japan. Now as they were still backstage.

Albert says; "Mary, sweetheart, it is so great that our dear friends, Anna Baby Love and her family can join us on our brief visit".

Anna Baby Love thanks Albert and Mary on stage; "you know thousands of people from the Philippines have traveled to Japan for this event, which is held in the world's largest auditorium. I am so awestruck by this outpouring of people to make a difference in the world energy.

ALBERT, you and your team are making such a powerful statement for all to hear".

The auditorium was packed with people and their restrained excitement was felt over the monitors.

Mary followed Anna by stating; "I feel the emotions of this wonderful group mind. It almost overwhelms me by all the thoughts that these people are having. Now **ALBERT,** I need your help to keep me grounded".

The team stood on the stage together radiating energy that the whole crowd felt. After introducing the rest of the team, Albert asks the crew;

"Bring the newly teleported Gateway onto the stage for all to see it. Everyone quiet please. Charles has the honor of activating The Gateway".

Without hesitation Charles playfully steps up for the task.

"Thank you for allowing me to start the Gateway spinning".

Just as in Australia, the Gateway put out a harmonic vibration that all could feel. The auditorium filled with white light that entered into each individual through the tops of their heads. Soon everyone was bathed with the white light and appeared to have a swirling egg shaped aura around them that healed all of their spirits' troubles. The light moved through their bodies and up through their heads again while continually bathing them with new light.

The white light circled the planet as everyone in the audience felt the spirit of the planet and every living thing on the planet as a part of each individual species. Then it moved out into space, leaving the Earth behind, looking like a marble in the heavens.

Looking back at the Earth, one could see the energy being radiating and the Earth looked like it was inside an egg. The egg had swirling colors of un-imaginable beauty. A healing of the planet seemed to be taking place as it did within the individuals, when the light first appeared in the auditorium.

Everyone knew that this could be felt across the universe as the light continued to travel further away from the Earth. Looking at the universe from an outside perspective, everyone could see life in abundance on many other planets in the galaxy. The light carried everyone outward, where they saw life at different stages of development in every galaxy they crossed.

Somehow everyone's consciousness felt that they were a part of all of this development throughout the universe and were transmitting new consciousness to all of these life forms. They could feel the light entering then leaving each planet with their consciousness shooting off in all directions to all corners of the never ending universe to find new realms. They traveled like the neurons in our mind, instantly going everywhere.

Soon after gleaning a brief glimpse of the universe surrounded in a luminescent egg or Taurus field, the renewed attendees began their journey back witnessing the energy all over again on smaller scales. The journey brought them back to the auditorium where the travelers journeyed within themselves to find they were made up of the same energy they saw everywhere. They saw waves of vibration and were filled with the emotion that could only be associated with love.

As the Gateway slowed and came to a stop, a new reality was awakened in everyone. They could feel the omnipresent that only a few had seen or experienced before in lifetimes.

Once again, the effects of this journey are unknown, however, without a doubt, nothing would ever be the same. The audience had touched the cosmic consciousness and realized their individual part in it.

The auditorium was quiet for a few more minutes, which seemed like an eternity. Then,

Albert was coughing as though to clear his throat; "Ah, hmm… We need to send the Gateway on to its next location. We have to keep on our schedule. Our team is moving on to China. Thank you so much for your wonderful reception of the Gateway".

Albert could not wait for the next surprise of the journey, which the Gateway would bring. So with excitement, the team got moving and sent the Gateway to the teleportation location.

Meanwhile, back in Borneo, BILL opened his suitcase after his brief nap and found they had a surprise stowaway with them.

"What have we here? **WISDOM?** What a surprise to have you hiding away like this. Come on out. Welcome".

WISDOM started looking around for Runner and the other mice. "Where's **RUNNER** and **BELCHOR**? This frantic search is useless, since we only found **SQUEAMISH** and **DAZZLER**. **SQUEAMISH**, where are **RUNNER** and **BELCHOR**"?

Squeamish assured them; "you will all see them soon. Just keep going as planned".

Still concerned that RUNNER and Belcher were missing, BILL, MYRA, BRANDON and SQUEAMISH began setting up for a display in Borneo's largest auditorium. DAZZLER helped in whatever way she could, even as she kept her eyes out for BELCHER and RUNNER.

The time had come for the festivities to begin. Suddenly, out on center stage the crowd saw on the monitors that the show had begun with two confused mice standing next to a cat. One of the mice was burping in spasms. The auditorium went wild with laughter as BILL and MYRA sighed with relief.

Myra stepped on stage; "laughter is the best way to start this event. Thank you. Our little entertainers are **RUNNER** and **BELCHER**. Today, we have the next step in our consciousness development. Enjoy the awakening".

The Gateway was brought in and BILL started it spinning. Again the Gateway calmed the auditorium with its pleasing humming vibration. With BILL's heightened power of observation, he noticed that this vision journey would take on even newer dimensions. As the people looked like a sea of light energy.

Waves of emotions could be felt, as visions of mankind in all stages of growth were swept into view showing all that mankind had done. Everyone could feel the unconscious greed of most individuals throughout history. The attendees saw, in a brief moment, how man had always lived off the energy of each other; taking selfishly for themselves without consideration for anything or anyone else. They felt the illusionary power of the controllers that seemed to have ruled for so long. The audience felt the oppression of the masses as these controllers used everything in their power to keep the illusion of control going for so many centuries.

The crowd felt the hunger of the starving as well as their will to survive. They cried as they saw how man mis-treated one another and the life giving planet called Earth. War disease, famine, lust, hatred, fear, sorrow, envy, jealousy, revenge, hopelessness and bitterness were experienced by all viewers. Then peace, healing, love, laughter, gratitude, cooperation,

sharing, awareness and caring for each other came in the next wave.

As each emotion was felt, images appeared to show the results that each had on the human development side. Each individual had their own images. BILL could see how energy changed with each wave. Everything was at first in darkness and then light took over the whole place. Gratefulness was felt within everyone as the light grew brighter. Puzzlement was also an overwhelming feeling as almost everyone realized, *we created all of the unnecessary bad feelings or darkness that stifled mankind*. Again gratitude took over as the feeling of puzzlement was swept away.

Realizations dawned as people became aware of how they had shaped their lives; on how they reacted with their emotions; the choices they made for their limited viewpoints for so long in their evolution. How people stole each other's energy to strengthen their own power just to survive over each other.

The realization that everyone lived in a universe made up of energy with abundance, brought back the feeling of puzzlement as to why we abused each other so much. Love then swept through the auditorium as the light got brighter within each consciousness never to go dark again in the same way. The next wave of darkness came with a new awareness that still allowed clarity even in the darkness. You could feel that both light and dark were a part of everyone and reactions to the darkness was a responsibility they all had to face and to make choices. Darkness was now just a backdrop that allowed the light to appear even brighter.

The Gateway slowly came to a stop with a revitalized awareness of everyone's conscious and unconscious decision-making. This reminder would renew all participants' determination to seek the light in the darkest of moments. All of these things are a part of the universe and how we choose to act. We must feel our emotions and have the capability to react in ways that will benefit the universe or each other.

BRAVO is talking to the mice below the bleachers. "WOW, I now think differently with this new understanding and compassion for the humans that we have feared for so long. I realize, we have more in common with the humans than any of us realized. I feel great. How about the rest of you, guys? I have such a new feeling of self-determination. Runner has informed me of what is going on and this goes all over the globe which is much larger than we could imagine. We need to tell more of our species and other species about this mice-triffick journey so they can have it also. Let's go and spread the word".

Laughter, music and dance spontaneously occurred with the feeling of relief that comes when you finally understand the darkness and choose the power of illumination. Once again the universe resounded with a vibration that healed everyone in all reaches of existence.

Mankind's made up world of illusions had vanished; a new paradigm of oneness was upon us. The electromagnetic field of the planet spiked "out of this world". All of creation reached a new height as a sickness had been cured.

Bill made an announcement before leaving the stage; "please, everyone, if possible, bring mice with you when you attend the tour events. Runner; bring your new friends to BRANDON if they wish to have the ability of communication with the hu-manes. You will have to tell us about your feline friend".

Runner responds; "that story will have to wait but I will do the introductions. This is PURR-PUSS the cat. BRAVO is one of the bravest mice I have met". "BRANDON will you start with PURR-PUSS"?

BRANDON touched PURR-PUSS on his left temple and then he had to step back.

"Reow, mewow; what was that"? "You leave my new friends alone". "What did you do"?

Runner scratched PURR-PUSS' head soothing him; "calm down kitty! Everything is alright! Now we can communicate as equals".

Bravo was next as Brandon helped many of the Borneo mice before the team moved on.

People attending the future stops brought their pet mice, if they had any. Pet outlets gathered their mice to send to the tour locations. An all-out attempt to gladly help the mice took place. This would bring about the evolution that SCOUT'S TRIBE desired without causing delays on the tour.

The people of the world reacted with such high positive action. Many other pets were also brought to the events. Dogs, cats, snakes, birds, and some people even rode their horses to the

events. This idea of promoting evolution within as many species as possible became the latest outpouring of love.

Bill comments to Myra; "I realize that the animals have helped many people to reach the state of love energy that would serve mankind best. This truly has a profound effect on the animal kingdom. This will be like the fruit from the tree of knowledge being given to the animals. The knowledge of the source within everything, along with the field that makes everything one, is powerful for all species. We are finally giving back to the animal kingdom in a big way".

CHAPTER 12

OPPOSITION EXPOSED

The dark cabal fine tunes their plans for the heist of the Gateway.

MILITARY MONGROL; "These first locations of the tour we'll use as a way of stalking the prize, The Gateway. These teleportation docks at each location are full of people awaiting the arrival of the Gateway. This will make our plans a little harder to pull off. Security is very tight; nevertheless, our dark forces have some security people working for us still, so this can be overcome".

RESOURCE RAPER; "They changed the job of the security personnel into a job of caring for loving individuals and no longer a revenue generating vampire on society. What a waste of resources. All our industries with the old mentality are close to obsolete, mainly because they were outsourced the work to honest commerce. I still can't believe it that most security personnel are there as watchers for the common good. These blinded people have developed themselves into the peak of awareness in the physical plain and many are in touch with the divine. We can't count on these reformed guards as their passion is to help mankind. However, we still have the clever few with ulterior motives that made it into the ranks of higher security. That will make this heist a success".

MISS DIS-INFORMATION; "The next few stops on the Gateway tour will give us the opportunity we need. China and Russia have many stops, while Vietnam only had one stop. The **ADRIAN** team is scheduled at the Vietnam stop. When the train arrives right on time, crowds will already be waiting at the station where the team is quickly ushered into the coliseum. A major distraction is planned to take place providing the opportunity for the switch".

The three hundred yards distance between the Coliseum and the teleportation dock. This is where the tube from one teleportation location to the other has only one brief stopping point. This stop is for verification. This point is where we plan to make our switch. Timing has to be precise".

> As usual, the teleportation dock was also crowded awaiting the arrival of the Gateway, which was expected momentarily. A replica of the Gateway had been engineered by the dark forces. It was already in position at the dock and in the hands of the operatives in South Vietnam.
>
> Upon the arrival of the Gateway, the fire alarms went off in the Coliseum. The Gateway was already in the teleport tube as pandemonium broke out in the crowd. Military Mongrel's sociopathic operatives were ready for the heist. The switch went off without a hitch. The thief was spotted leaving the tube's stopping point. Before he was stopped the thief quickly hid the real Gateway in a nearby trash bin. A well-centered, observant guard found nothing suspicious; they let him go; continuing to watch him as he left their proximity. The plan was being pulled off without a hitch. The cleaning robots would bring the trash to the disintegrating dump where it would be retrieved by the cabal minions.

> It only took a few moments for the alarms to be turned off, as everyone realized there was no fire. The event excitement returned quickly to the people. The bogus Gateway was brought out after a brief introduction of ADRIAN, PENNY and the rest of their team.

ADRIAN gives a moment of meditation before starting the Gateway spinning

Everyone, join me in a silent moment to set your intention of what you desire to receive from this moment of revelation. **(silent moment)**

> **Nothing happened when the Gateway spinning activation started. There was no soothing harmonic frequency or any lights at all. A wave of disappointment reverberated through the coliseum; however, everyone's spirits remained high over all.**
>
> **ADRIAN stops the spinning replica.**

"Let me examine the Gateway as something is very wrong here. This is clearly not the Gateway. I see the treasure inscription engraved on the rim is missing. This is not the real Gateway. It is a replacement. We must find the Gateway now".

"Kind Audience, our, **SCOUT, JASMINE** and **BABBLER** tracked the Gateway, when it was sent to USE, our center. So, my wonderful **TRIBE**, tune in with the vibration that the Gateway continually emits. Find our Gateway.

> **The TRIBE members took off in a purposeful direction without saying a word with 8 year old PENNY right behind them. The mice headed to the trash bin hiding the Gateway. The mice pointed and jumped frantically at the trash bin, trying to get in it. The custodian robots moved towards the bin to get to the Gateway first. Their programming had been altered making them aggressive. They chased the mice around with**

their broom attachments while one of them grabbed the bin and headed towards the service exit.

Scout hurries Penny; "over here, it's in there; stop that gadget.

Penny spilled her soap bubbles on the smooth marble floor in front of the bot. The custodian bot slid into a pillar where it dropped the trash bin. Penny detached the power chip from the fleeing robot. Then Penny helped open the trash bin.

Jasmine ran back to Adrian bursting with pride; "Our **TRIBE** found the Gateway intact".

Adrian broadcasted to the world; "these mice are once again the heroes of the day and the stars of this show".

> There was only a five minute delay on the schedule. This activation would certainly be unique from all the others so far. Numerous different emotions were felt by everyone before the activation even got started. The people returned to their heart centers quickly with the celebration of happiness at the safe rescue of the Gateway.
>
> As the spinning started, you could feel the flow of the past moments reach a calm that pooled into the collective consciousness, before reaching a downstream movement again. A spiral or vortex of light encompassed the whole area leading up into the sky. This vortex was acting like a receiver of the cosmic consciousness from our galactic family.
>
> All attendees were like babies looking up at their mother for the very first time. Trust was instinctive because of this loving energy. It felt like being cradled in the arms of existence, nurtured by the miracle of life. The light spiral went away like an umbilical cord being cut as humanity was born again with all the knowledge of past lives. Our purpose for being here was revealed not only on an individual basis, but also as

a species. We are co-creators in the ever changing universe as we all move closer to the source of creation. Somehow we all knew that we were finally on our own, as well as part of an even greater whole. We were realizing our true selves as individual self-motivating beings with purposes.

The unique collective awareness of humanity became more apparent as our connection to the galactic consciousness stream came with a new acceptance. Better yet, we were reminded of our responsibility to create rather than destroy. Creating and co-existence is what brings out our happiness, so we must nurture this.

This activation ended leaving the crowd content in just being present. The overwhelming feeling of love could be felt over the world. Forgiveness though was tapered with caution as the tour continued with only a minimal delay, despite the efforts and the dark intentions of the few.

Foiled again, the cabal meet, possible for the last time.

MILITARY MONGROL; "with the added security at the next locations we will not deter our intentions. Making further attempts at taking the Gateway may be difficult. We just have to recalibrate our plans for our next efforts. Too bad our plans are out in the open now for all to recognize. Any future snatch will no longer be as easy as it was there in Vietnam. Let's plan wisely...."

All the air was out of dark cabals balloon. For the remainder of the tour, most attempts at taking the Gateway at each location were easily spotted and stopped. With one exception!

China was the next stop, where there were just as many animals present as there were people. Just about every species imaginable was represented: pandas, lizards, thousands of mice, even elephants, lions, giraffes and many more. The activation would take place in a valley surrounded by flat top mountains, where millions could participate in the great sharing. The valley was created by an ancient meteor strike hundreds of thousands of years ago. The sky above this area was lit with stars that seemed to shine brighter than usual. There were only a few scattered buildings in this valley, because the inhabitants wanted to be as close to nature as they could get. So having the event in the city was not even considered.

> This was another first for mankind having this large a gathering in one location. Nothing previous to this event even came close to the numbers attending. Even with the mass numbers there, everyone was mindful of the earth and vowed to not harm the valley. Everyone vowed to leave the valley better off when they have all left. Many brought seedlings for fruit trees, pines, oaks, bamboo and many more varieties of plant life to be planted before they leave. This was their way of giving back to the earth for allowing them to gather here.

> People would come back to this valley for years to nurture this new paradise. The seedlings planted were said to be blessed with the Gateway activation so everything growing there had cosmic nurturing. The fruits from the trees that would grow had cleansing for the body that brought one back to their natural physical wellbeing. This was the earth giving back to us.

> This planting of trees also added another common practice along the tour. Most of the events were scheduled in outdoor locations as China's conscious concern for our environment only made sense. Most of the locations were left more pristine than they were before the events. Many of the animals remained behind at these location to assist in creating gardens of immense beauty.

> Mankind was getting used to leaving any space they occupied, within reality, better with more potential growth and positive

energy. This new collective awareness brought life, not destruction, along our path. Even the broken pieces of society began to flourish. This mindset had been present in man's development. It was now blossoming with beneficial fruit as the majority of the world now embraced this new concept.

In Russia, The first stop had some unique occurrences also. This was also an outdoors event near the world's largest manmade Sea Aquarium. Russia had built a large lake about one hundred square miles in diameter at this inland location. A geological survey had shown the presence of tremendous natural granite barrier over one hundred feet below sea level. This natural barrier allowed Russian engineers to excavate well below sea level without being flooded. Before filling the lake, they built Plexiglas domed Walkways with large gathering areas along the bottom of this great project. They then tapped into a nearby tunnel that lead out into the ocean. Geo-thermal heaters were installed to keep the temperature of the water close to tropical water.

The center building within this great lake reached two hundred feet above the surface of the lake with a panoramic view that was hard to match. This was where the Gateway Activation was to take place. This location was not only out in nature but it was under water. The shore line around the lake held millions of spectators as well. This was the largest gathering representation of all living species on earth.

The lake was full of dolphin, stingrays, sharks and just about any sea life one could imagine. Endangered species had safe habitats to restore their numbers. It was like a sanctuary for all endangered sea life. Populations Schools of fish would be nurtured back into prosperity then re-introduced into the world waterways.

The Dolphins were already highly conscious beings along with many other sea animals. The awareness of this coming event was well known and greatly anticipated by the dolphins. When the Gateway got activated, they all swam in the same direction circling the observation building. This caused a vortex in the water that opened another Gateway to the core of the earth.

> Within the very center of the Earth, the universe or the Source existed just like it existed within our heart center and everything else. Orbs of light lit up the waters and if you looked closely enough you could see figures inside the center of the orbs. They danced around in unison displaying many color from the light spectrum. Multi-dimensional entities made their presence known to humanity at this event. Now that the dolphins had opened this other Gateway, the dolphins would be freer to show themselves or, to put it another way, the people could now see them in their true spirit.
>
> What looked like angels (best way to describe them) descended from the sky holding hands forming a huge circle around the event while the dolphins jumped out of the water to greet them! The darkness of the evening only made the sources of light more visible to all the cameras that recorded this miracle for the rest of the planet to view. It takes darkness for us to really see the light. This is the purpose the dark cabal used to

control humanity. The light always overwhelms the darkness and many have been slow in realizing this or how this pertains to existence.

Each Gateway activation seemed to outdo the previous one. This did not matter because it was a constant stream broadcast to the rest of the world. Everyone was given powers this day; the power to see, hear, smell, taste and feel with these five senses well beyond their normal capacity.

Our other senses were opened up and heightened as well. They are much more numerous than the limiting 5 senses we relied on in our past. What many people would have considered super powers or super abilities are now becoming common place within the global community.

ALBERT makes a comment on the world broadcast network; "the Gateway is just the catalyst that the world needs to unite us in a positive united consciousness. Humanity is reaching its potential just by gathering with loving intentions".

This was truer than ALBERT imagined. As the world tour continued this would become even clearer to the collective awareness of humanity. The animals exposed to the activations were also displaying signs of evolution. The give and take of natural order underwent a dramatic shift. The animal kingdom would never be the same as so many animals were already aware of the cycle of life. The strong living off the weaker species, that many people thought was the order of things, was exposed to be a farce.

Animals were aware that they had to give back more than they took from life; way before the Gateway exposure. What seemed like primitive, savage behavior of killing for survival, held more civilized behavior, than the humans who killed for many other reasons? The history of humanity held more primitive behavior than any animal species had known.

Even the sharks of the world knew about humans and their destructive path. The sharks even had a sense of cosmic balance that man did not possess or ignored for thousands of years. Even piranhas did not attack to eat their own kind.

The animals could feel the change in the human species, they had feared. They were changed by the harmonic vibration of love that was being shared around the planet. They would have felt this change even without being exposed to the Gateway activations. Our negative energy as a species had affected the animals for many, many life cycles.

The spectacular sea aquarium stop in Russia concluded with the planting of trees around the shoreline and leaving this location full of wonderful prospects for others to reap benefits for years to come.

Mankind's stewardship of planet Earth was taking on an even newer level of higher co-existence with all species. This level had never been reached anywhere in the known cosmos. Thus, it set an example for other worlds to follow. These changes were now happening on a galactic, multi-dimensional scale. The flapping of an emerging butterfly's wings was generating energy on a cosmic level.

CHAPTER 13

CONSCIOUSNESS DENSITY

As the tour continued, Albert was visited by the guide, Zeb, who asked him if he could speak through him to the world population. Albert agreed. Then Albert made preparation for this unusual broadcast.

This would take place on the train were there were no distractions. Mary and Charles helped with setting up this surprise event.

The team formed a tight semi-circle with Albert and Mary in the middle looking towards the main camera. All that Albert had to do was close his eyes and Zeb was with him. Albert once again gave Zeb permission to speak through him.

Zeb began by saying, "Inhabitants of Planet Earth, I come to you now to share with you visions of the changes that have taken place recently, looking from an outside perspective. This sharing is playful in nature with knowing that it will bring more clarity to those that need it."

"Density is the distance of sub-atomic particle from other sub-atomic particles. It is the closeness of these particles that create mass or objects. No object can exist without sub-atomic particles that are made up of ninety percent space. From a distance, even particles that are far apart look like one object."

As Zeb spoke, a three dimensional image of our solar system appeared in front of the group, only it was not being projected by any devices in the train car. The Gateway was not with them and this was happening anyway.

Pointing to the third planet from the sun, Zeb continued, "This is your home as it looked just recently. You will be viewing a time lapse progression to the here and now. What you will be shown is using many spectrums along with different frequencies. This is how earth is being viewed and the spectacular experience it is providing the universal grid connecting to all sources. These things could not be observed using limited senses. The sound you hear is the sound coming from your planet that is adjusting for you to hear it."

The sounds of birds singing, the waves washing to shore and water falling could be heard in the background as Zeb continued his sharing, "As you see your planet looked very normal until the early 20th Century in your way of calculating time. First you will notice a flicker where the light of your planet was almost extinguished. Then your brightness began to grow. This is where we return to the subject of density".

"Energy beings from far and wide wondered *what had happened that caused the dimming*, so they began to investigate. The planet was already on watch because of its use of atomic weapons and other harmful ways of destruction. Notice, when our visitations started in greater numbers, your planet appeared to grow or take on the shape of a new object. This could not be seen by you even with your developing technology".

"What our investigators observed, upon arrival, was a struggling world without balance. Many of these visitors began strengthening the light wherever they saw the need for it and others attempted to extinguish any light they came across".

"The majority of your world had plenty of indigenous light beings; yet many light beings were allowing themselves to be suppressed by a few darker spirits. The Galactic Council stopped outside influence then and began just observing".

"What you have accomplished here at this time, you did with minimal help or interference from our species. You had to become aware of something more than something outside yourself. That you knew you were a part of something, and then had to realize that your connection is within yourself before asking for help. The help you got came to you on your own merits with just little reminders or hints from your Galactic family".

"The shape of your planet continued to grow as you bought your light out from within yourself. This became a steady change and growth until just a moment ago, in time space, where you will see your planet become one of the brightest stars in your galaxy. A star made up of conscious density serving as a beacon within existence. This sharp rise in intensity occurred before your Gateway tour began. It was your mass agreement to return to your heart centers that caused this wonderful spectacle that I am sharing with you. You have set an example for all species to follow without the use of any outside stimulus such as the Gateway. What you experienced now with the activations is like watering a healthy plant that will make full use of the additional nourishment."

The train car was lit up by the amazing display that was being shared by Zeb. Our Earth was larger than any object around, while the natural field that kept the solar system in place went undisturbed. The added mass was not matter as we know it or even atmosphere, it was best described as light, independent light sources like pixels' in a photograph.

Zeb continued, "Very few planets reach this level of connection with source. This has created something new within the being one might call 'the one universal conscious awareness' that is, in turn, a part of something even bigger, individual, conscious awareness".

"You are now at the beginning of your own self-development in a new realm created with love, by you, for you and for all you come in contact with. You are free to visit the cosmic consciousness whenever you chose, free to go wherever you please as part of the Galactic family. You have earned your sovereignty with the heavens, by becoming a star. The quarantine of your planet is lifted, soon you will join the Galactic Council".

"Enjoy your celebrations. Realizing that creation on its continual progression is celebrating with you. May your light grow even brighter!" concluded Zeb.

With this sharing completed, the display went away as Albert returned feeling refreshed.

"Thank you, Zeb," Mary commented, "We are grateful for the wisdom you shared. We are on a miracle wave that has unlimited positive effects."

Meanwhile, the tour was still at the beginning of its way around the globe. Time had passed so quickly that the teams were half way around the planet before taking a moment just for them. This was important as a daily ritual for most people and these teams deserved their time alone. This is a moment of just being or the appreciation of just being. It brings a second wind to each individual that helps the day along. The teams would need this centering for what lay ahead.

With events planned in India, Pakistan, Yemen, and throughout the Asian countries, everything went smoothly. This region is now called Persia once again. The division that took place was an illusion that disappeared with the removal of imaginary borders. The maps were even missing the imaginary lines that were "drawn in the sand" so to speak.

The people all brought and shared many new things at the events. In Iraq, there was a celebration for the return to one language of

love that could be understood by everyone. Quantum language (the correct mathematical language) could be translated to all languages with the same meaning. Things had come full circle for this region of our planet. Where separation started (for whatever reason) is where it also ended.

The universal language of numbers and geometry was developing new comprehensions constantly. Quantum language (the language of correctness) has brought truth out from behind the veils of illusion. Trust, treaties, Constitutions, Documents, contracts, declarations and any other agreement were made with full closure. Ancient scripts never released before were brought out to be shared with the world. Guarded secrets became common knowledge. Other stargates around the world were opened. Some of these stargates were not even discovered by humanity, yet it became clear who had discovered them when they opened. Many light beings already knew that we are all stargates ourselves as this became common knowledge as things progressed.

A new closure was happening on a global scale. The wealth of knowledge had opened the flood gates as nothing that would help or bring value was held back. Our drive to improve creation as co-creators was elevated by our willingness to share. The genius of mankind was shared; so every solution that now had a problem, was coming up with newer solutions making possibilities grow exponentially. Our minds were now working together without competition or ego and centered on the common good for all. Prosperity has taken on a whole new understanding.

The release of self-sustaining individual energy technology for each structure, in the year 2013, helped bring about the solutions needed in that troubling time. By breaking the dependency on the grid energy system, along with the dependency on oil that was built around the profit paradigm, held massive support to those with the power of self-determination. Almost everything produced now has its own power source; so electric power grid systems are no longer needed. It was the creative power of self-determination that caused the economic boom for this planet. Each journey begins with our first step.

While Bill and Myra's team was finishing up in Africa on their last stop, before crossing the Atlantic, they participated in another activation of dramatic proportions.

The Morocco tour stop was at an inlet off the Atlantic Ocean capable of holding millions around the surrounding cliff. The waters of the ocean were deep, azure blue. The inlet had a large coral reef protection that stretched for miles out to sea which broke up the waves coming in to shore. These were some of the most beautiful waters in the world that were quickly returning to their natural state after many centuries of misuse. The whole planet continued recovering from our past learning experiences that ushered in the last consciousness shift in 2012 through 2015. This shift towards co-existence will still be taking place for a while within many individuals.

The significance of this location is that the reefs are believed to be the buildings from a suburb of sunken Atlantis. Many of the Atlantian spirits were still in this area, attached to this density to live out the lessons they needed to learn. This was like a parole for them to experience completion. These spirits would not miss this opportunity. The ocean animals all seemed to be aware of this gate opening, so the waters were abundant with life never seen before in such numbers.

Everything was being rejuvenated on a microscopic cellular level that radiated outward giving new life to the biological life beings that comprised the living object they were part of, such as the coral in the reefs glowed, freely giving life force energy to the waters.

The sky above was like a blue marble with wispy white clouds all scurrying around so to not miss anything. When the Gateway got activated, these clouds started moving in a circular motion creating a funnel that touched the water. This was not like experiencing a storm. The birds flocked to the funnel flying with the direction of the winds. This funnel went from the sky down to the ocean then inverted from the Earth upward. The closest one could come to describing it would be nature's giving and receiving strength. It looked like a funnel cake pan with the center spiraling up into the universe.

The living sea took on the same shape only downward into the center of the Earth and skyward on the outer circle. A beam of violet purple light lit up the center then disappeared into the universe. You could see thousands of souls rising up within the violet beam, each giving off their own light. The early morning sky had displayed a brightness that was believed to be the anxious Galactic family waiting to greet their long lost relatives. These multi-density relatives were swooping down to pick up their family members, whisking them up into the stars.

The spirits of Inner Earth also gathered up their long, imprisoned relatives taking them home to the source within Mother Earth, thus back to the one Creator. This did not stop when the Gateway stopped spinning because it was a separate occurrence. The two events happened with synchronicity in harmony with each other. The harvesting of souls would last for hours.

One could feel the exultation everywhere; bringing an even greater reason to celebrate. Monumental changes were occurring on an hourly basis giving a new meaning to time. The "here" encompassed everything and the "now" encompassed all time.

As the tours finished in Africa and Europe, the teams were heading towards the Americas, stories were shared by everyone. Many of the stories would also be left untold, yet the significance of these stories will be just as important at a later time. Where were you on Independence Day in the year 2035?

CHAPTER 14

DREAM REALITY

On the way across the Atlantic in wrought to the America the teams all had a brief rest. Albert pondered to himself the short history of the settling of this land.

"I realize that the Americas were not only built from the dreams of our ancestors but also from the dreams of the indigenous people who were possibly the closest to the divine creator before intervention from old Europe began".

"Those dreams, the indigenous people had, were eventually manifested into this society where we are now. A great asking for forgiveness was still needed for the atrocities that had occurred by the early settlers from the European countries and early colonies. This asking could only come from the individual heart center because the mouth had proven to be un-truthful in the past. Remember that old saying of the Indians, 'He speaks with forked tongue'."

Hearing Albert's thoughts, Mary replies using her telepathic ability; "now we are seeing this asking for forgiveness take place at every location along this Gateway tour, here in the Americas, especially

THE UNITED STATES, who is just now admitting to any fault. Recognition of past in-humane deeds is the first step to forgiveness. It feels so good".

The conversation continued without words being spoken, Albert; "you are so right, **MARY**". "The acceptance of this heart filled asking for forgiveness is also needed for true healing of past injustices. On a galactic scale, this is the time. It sure took a while for this to happen because many individuals felt it was **not** their generation that perpetrated this inhuman injustice; so they did not need to ask for forgiveness. Meanwhile, with the new awareness of existence being shown around the world, everyone has started to see the wound was still open and only the present generation can close it. Oh, I am so glad I am here to see it happening".

Benn mouse took a while to become comfortable but he was somehow aware of this mental conversation taking place.

"The mice have started this forgiveness wave by re-establishing their place in the universe without needing validation from anyone. Now we can reach out to our former oppressors with love"!

"This is a surprise hearing you", Mary thought! "Yes, Benn, this American dream had taken many shapes for many people turning into horrible nightmares for many. The reality shapers with dreams of a united free society got mixed in with the tyranny of control beings who distorted things to reach their own selfish intent. The best way to destroy a dream is from within the dream. We certainly saw the fruits of that idea at the closing of 2011".

Albert explained to Benn; "only those that learned how to control their dream reality could gain control in the third dimensional world, were finally able to accept the results as a prime reality. I remember earlier times when all those who could dream on their own or acted on their dreams were stifled, all for a concept called manifest destiny. In the meantime, the dreams of freedom were kept alive as an illusion to cover up the bondage into which the powers that were had sold the people".

"**ALBERT,** dear, I remember you telling me it took dreamers to break this strangle hold on the masses that were being programmed by a handful of controllers. In 2011, the global financial system was realized to be flawed an illusion at its best in favor of negative, self-centered people with little regard for anything, only themselves. Fraud, greed, lust, draconian behavior was rewarded in this backwards society. Some of those seeking control had good intentions in some ways. They knew that one had to show self-determination and free will to have the gift of true freedom. They felt that they were the catalyst for the change".

"So they created a new form of slavery to test one's resolve. This psychological game was not understood by many who served their role in ensuring control.

These minions were actually serving their own ego with an illusion of control. This illusion had to be accepted as reality by the masses for the leaders that were to have any true authority. They took the power from the people, therefore, when the people stopped giving the game players' power, the players could not survive any more on their own abilities. The game was all based on consent, implied or un-implied. Once you withdrew your consent, you also withdrew the life force sustaining energy of the illusion. Even in our ignorance, we unknowingly possessed the power of the so called gods. Once mankind became aware of this ability, the masses would only consent to that which served the well being of all mankind, not brotherhoods, banks, secret societies, corporations or governments".

"You hu-manes have gone through some tough lessons", Benn thought. "These are thought provoking ideas of freedom as being continuously earned by your knowledge of who you are and your connection to the divine source. Our **TRIBE** learned that no other being is more important than you and you are no better than they are. We have always used the concept of what you call self-governance and saw that for you to learn self-governance you cannot live place in a realm of dependence. When we were attempting to get your attention, it was our lesson we learned that when someone possesses something you think you need for prosperity or survival and they dangle it in front of you, you have to accept the fact that they are the owners for them to gain the upper hand over you. Without your acceptance they have no authority. Our **TRIBE** used the dark day to make our survival work for us. It was something you needed to learn as we watched you. We never gave consent to you, hu-manes".

"Wow, **Benn**, you said that so well", Albert was amazed. "Now here in the Americas there was a mixture of concepts that were still being developed. It took the dark cabal to allow the light to shine brighter. Light shines brighter in darkness. It took them to show us what freedom really was for all people. We no longer need the dark energies to find the light".

Sharing Albert's amazement, Mary adds. "Yes, understanding this concept is very critical as to how the Gateway has affected the people around the world".

The first activation in the Americas took place in the New York area, it took the form of past and present dreams. Generations of dreamers emerged in one dreamscape as if they were all attending the event. It was powerful.

> The Gateway was spinning in the middle of a ceremonial circle made up of things that represented the four major elements of Air, Water, Earth and Fire. Spirits of great shamans appeared in the sky overlooking these events. The universe was again displayed for all to witness. This time the universe appeared in many layers as if it had millions of reflections on top of each other. Each layer had its own existence and appeared to be just one possible reality among millions.
>
> In one reality portrayed, the indigenous people and the settlers lived and worked with each other so no genocide ever took place. This new consciousness reality had been reached long ago, while the higher densities are just now being

reached. This energy is making its way through each plane of existence having different effects on each person. Our new unique energy can mix with this expansive flow to become even greater synergy.

Within the dream state you can travel from one plain of existence to another, the quantum jumping skill. You can become yourself in other plains to learn from your expert double what you may not know in your reality. Within the dream state you can also visit past reincarnations or even future reincarnations of yourself. Just about anything is possible in the dream state with the only limitations being the ones you create for yourself.

Here at these Gateway events, you can do all the things that you could do in a dream state, only now it is in the state of wakefulness. Other versions of people and species from different levels and planes are also visiting these events through the one's physically in attendance.

This doorway between realities has never been opened in such a large scale before these events. The fact that most attendees have tapped into their own child within or their heart center allowed for this overall positive experience. Dark, harmful emotions, that normally cause nightmares were present, nevertheless those emotions were overwhelmed by the overall good emotions being felt by all the masses.

The animals present at the Gateway activation participated in the dream visions as well. Horses remembered their lives as eagles; mice remembered their lives as cats, the elephant, someone bought in, remembered his life as a mouse and as a wolf. Some animals remembered their lives as humans.

All that one had to do was ask a question and they would instantly go to the best place in existence to get their answer.

As in all the activations, each individual had their own unique experience within the journeys.

The comprehension of what we are all here to accomplish had individual meanings to each person. Some needed to learn lessons, some needed to heal old wounds, and some are here to help others that they love as much as they love themselves be able to receive these gifts. There are too many reasons to list. What became increasingly clear was that the collective consciousness is about getting closer to source creator through the love vibration.

Mary, Albert and Benn continued their mental conversation after the New York event. Mary started by noting; "I noticed that some of the people attending the event, their eyes were moving at a fast rate in all directions, similar to R.E.M. sleep that takes place while dreaming. Their eyes were wide open even though you could see the reflections of the multi-universe in their eyes. They may not even see you looking at them, because you are not participating in their reality. I was able to visit so many of the people during our events. It was very revealing to me".

"In our species", Benn was sharing; "there was still some who did not open themselves up for this experience who remained in the third density only seeing a good light show with a bunch of people acting weird. They had a purpose of grounding the others to third density even if they were unaware of the role they played. Even though they were unable to allow the full experience they knew that no harm would come to anyone so they had their own good time. I realized that they will have a delayed reaction as we had with our **TRIBE**. You and **MARY** helped us so much with your love and respect of our slower capacities at that first time. So we must also allow that for our many species that did not make that jump".

The Gateway was removed by one of the trusted contributors to take to the teleportation dock. The next scheduled location for the

Activation was in Brazil, where ADRIAN's team was set to host that particular event.

At the teleportation dock, they did not know that the coordinates of the transfer had been changed. Brazil immediately announced that the Gateway did not arrive as planned. An expert teleportation programmer was brought in to determine where it had gone. It took several minutes to bring in the specialist and even longer for him to determine the location. Precious time was being lost. After due diligence, the answer presented itself, the Gateway was in the District of Columbia, the old capital of the US.

A recovery team was immediately dispatched which included CHEEZER, CRACKER and BENN who were the closest ones to the DC district. ALBERT was also part of the recovery team.

Information on the exact location was pin pointed so security moved in ahead of the arrival of ALBERT's team. When security searched the site the Gateway was nowhere to be found. Evidence of it being there was discovered near the teleportation devise. The perpetrators could have taken it anywhere then teleported it again. At this point they needed expert trackers. The global sensitivity of the Gateway's presence was heightened within many because the best hope was with the collaboration of mice and man.

When CHEEZER, CRACKER and BENN arrived on the scene, they immediately went to work. It only took a few moments for them to feel a vibration pulling them in one direction.

Cracker; "this way". Come on, this way. Let's hurry".

ALBERT's anti-gravity vehicle followed his friends' directions to the letter leading them to the Washington Monument, where they were greeted by armed security with a different motive.

Right behind ALBERT was a force of protectors and media that had followed the hunter mice. This had become a global media blitz that could end in galactic shame. One of the dark cabal minions spoke out,

MINNI MIND **angrily;** "we have no idea where your Gateway is now. Only the CEOs would know and they have all gone home. You only have the words of some mice that it was ever here. So good luck with that!!! No one here had anything to do with your missing object".

Cheezer nodded; "they are right, it is no longer here".

Benn and Cracker agreed; "**CHEEZER** is correct. It is not far away though.

ALBERT, it's close to that park over there".

In the park, they found a small building that was run down and fenced off. This building was surrounded by a dense forest and could not be seen until entering the small forest. Nothing looked out of the ordinary. So they proceeded cautiously into the abandoned structure. The mice ran to a hatch in the floor which Albert opened. Flashlights showed a ladder leading down to a large room with an elevator.

Albert felt drawn to this location as well; "I feel we're being watched. Since the others are following right behind us to help out if we are confronted by anything. I also feel that we are being invited to enter". "How strange"!!!!!

They all went down the ladder. ALBERT pushed the elevator button and the doors opened immediately. ALBERT, CHEEZER, CRACKER and BENN stepped into the elevator, even knowing that backup might have a hard time following their progress.

A moment later, they stopped and the doors opened into what appeared to be a large underground city. The group was greeted in a diplomatic manner by several well-dressed ambassadors that led them to a large chamber filled with the most advanced computers available in ALBERT's understanding. In the middle of the chamber, awaiting Albert's arrival, were several distinguished members sitting at a round table that showed a display board.

As Albert and his team approached they heard,

KIND HEART was speaking; "we did not mean for any harm to come to anyone. We had need of your Gateway in our city. We are a hidden part of your world where only a selected few of our kind come or go to your surface. These few have worked their way into your system; however, their first obligation is to us. Your dark, intentioned, want-to-be rulers that controlled your failed corporate government no longer exist. We had stayed around to keep a new uprising from occurring in the dustbins of history. The want-to-be rulers served their purpose by displaying what happens in a society that is ruled by outside authority. Where you should have been nurturing the power of self-determination, your masses choose the easy way of listening to those outside authorities to their own detriment".

HISTORY HEART went on; "many of our tribes came here for refuge as the outsiders that came from across the waters started war on our land. We are mixed with star beings that are aware of the senseless need for violence. Our heritage needed to be preserved. Once here, we choose to stay to build on our own environment, unhindered by outside influences. We have prospered for generations until your Twentieth Century. This is when we started being affected by surface dwellers pollution. Our water became poisoned, our ground became barren. Our influence in your surface world had to move forward with positive intent so we became peaceful warriors behind the scenes. We played a hidden role in your great paradigm shift".

KIND HEART assured Albert; "you can take the Gateway with you, once we activate it in our city. This activation is about to take place, if you will join us".

Albert agrees; "I will be honored to start The Gateway".

The city exploded with radiant light that reached every corner of this vast underground city. Beings of all styles stepped out into the light bathing in it with laughter and song. The sounds reverberated throughout the underground cavern causing the stalactite to vibrate, adding to the song. This mixture of sound and light opened a spherical rift in the space that expanded filling the cavern. Inside the sphere, you could feel the unconditional love of the source creator. The waters cleaned up and new vegetation sprouted out of the ground. The sphere, made out of collected star material, started to shrink, leaving the highest part of the cavern illuminated like daytime.

The Gateway stopped on its own.

> Then ALBERT, CHEEZER, CRACKER and BENN were escorted back to the elevator with the Gateway in hand. As they departed, they all took one last look at the city and were amazed at the spectacular view of this marvelous city now restored to its pristine state.
>
> A crowd of frantic people were waiting at the elevator doors. With an honor guard, the Gateway went to the nearest teleportation dock to continue its journey. No one was discouraged that over three hours had been lost on the tour schedule. Albert told the story of what had happened.

Speaking to the global audience Albert told them; "once again the mice are heroes for leading us in the right direction. The people of the Underground environment are with us all the way and have restored their homes to a healthy living for everyone there. We honor their commitment to being part of our evolution and great love for all species. We never knew they existed before this detour. Thank you all for your support and love to bringing this side trip to a happy ending".

The people cheered for their return. Everyone was pleased that whatever time was lost helped the newly discovered underground inhabitants that were previously harmed by the dark cabal.

Albert added; "this was not the work of the confused dark cabal. I believe the dark cabal will leave us alone for the rest of the tour as it is way too late in the game for those former powers that were, to affect the outcome of today's events".

CHAPTER 15

LEADING TO THE GRAND FINALE

The Grand Finale was to take place in Hawaii with the convergence of all the teams. Most all of South, Central and North America's events took place despite the delays that happened in New York and old DC. Each event held its own unique significance. The events located in Peru and also in the Four Corners of New Mexico, Arizona, Utah and Colorado in the US had great significance.

The Four Corners are where many sacred places have their own unique energy on our planet. A ceremony would take place along with the activation that would evoke healing energy for the planet. Many ceremonies in past histories were believed to be superstitious by some of the inhabitants. Now mankind has learned there is a science behind what occurs during these ceremonies. Depending on the type of ceremony being performed and the intent of the ritual will lead to any given results. Intent is what makes any ceremony positive or negative, constructive or destructive, value creation or value destroyer.

These Four Corners events helped the most as they held more people than any previous event in the Americas. The team had time to cancel some of the West Coast events and take those people to the Four Corners.

All of the northern hemisphere's indigenous nations of the Turtle Island were at this Four Corners event. Turtle Island is what the Americas were called before the migration from the European countries.

Albert addressed the travelers; "team, we are being met at the train station by a group of Shaman. The grandmothers are also among the elders. What an honor that is for us to have such wonderful aged wisdom propel The Gateway forward with our brethren".

"First we will hear from GRANDMOTHER DESTINY".

Grandmother Destiny spoke for the group. She had a bubbly energy field that soothed while energizing those around her. "Some of our ceremonies do the same thing that the Gateway does in that they open doors into parallel dimensions, multiple-universes and different densities. Alternative reality is recognized and interacted with other modalities. These are tools of any great shaman, who easily comprehend the scientific mind when looking from a quantum level. Geometry, astronomy and all the sciences are linked to the universe; available to the opened mind".

"What takes place at our events will stifle the scientific mind that is stuck on conclusive evidence based on theory, then testing. Very simply put; all things we know or accept as reality are made from the density and composition of sub-atomic particles, plus our acceptance or agreement that something exists. By affecting the sub-atomic worlds, you are affecting matter in our density making things, such as shape shifting, levitation, invisibility, molecular construction drawn from surrounding elements and many other abilities possible".

"There are also different ways that one could learn these abilities also, as an example, one can become invisible by bending light around oneself or by changing density or by taking your physical body to another location or even by vibrating at a frequency just out of range to the normal five senses. Shape shifting can take place by bringing into this density another version of you as a bird in the multi-verse or by actually changing your molecules and cells into reshaping themselves".

Albert injected a passing thought; "this background information will help many that are struggling with the total destruction of their old paradigms. What has been happening around the world for the past few days has caused anxiety to those that were not ready. So they sought believable explanations for all the miracles they were witnessing! Instead of allowing or embracing, they were explaining or justifying"!

Grandmother Destiny continued; "people, with many already new and existing abilities, are attending these Four Corner events knowing of the special connection to earth consciousness this area holds. From all over the globe, people come, even if they had attended a previous activation. They knew this one would hold a special significance for them".

"Some will observe miracles happening to others. Some choose to experience the event by assuming the shape of one of their guiding spirits and changed into eagles, hawks, wolves, many other forms were familiar and some unfamiliar".

"Food and nourishment will be supplied for everyone by those who can pull the elements right out of the atmosphere to create what they intended".

Skywise one of the other elders; "the sky is full of spaceships from all around the galaxies. Source energy is permeating through and around everything. The earth itself is shape shifting. You can feel tremors reverberating underneath. They pose no threat because they are an energy wave passing dark energy off the planet then returning as balanced light. For the cosmic entity housing, we all called Earth; it is like a brief chill with cosmic goose bumps. Mother Earth has been going through the same changes the inhabitants are now experiencing.

Mother Earth feels the great love being generated by her conscious co-creators whom she has nurtured and loved for so long".

Grandmother Destiny finished up; "the overall consciousness of the planet is made up of billions of individual, conscious singularities. All are granted the gift of free will to give their gift away to others, which makes others more powerful if you allow it. The choice one makes either has beneficial effects or detrimental effects. So the indigenous species of a planet learn to move closer to the divine by making creative, beneficial choices. Thus, the whole planet's consciousness rises to new levels. This in turn is shared throughout existence to encourage all things to seek closeness with the Creator Source. The choices that we, as a species, make on any planet; determines not only the reality in which they live but also the health of the planet on which they live. Planets are seeking source as well".

Albert was grateful for the wisdom sharing; "Thank you, Great Elders for your insights and observation delivered to us before stepping up to this activation platform. We are humbled by your great sharing".

The Gateway activation started with everyone holding their intent towards healing our home. Asking Mother Earth for forgiveness for all of the thoughtless abuse man has caused in their development and was being accepted by this loving entity.

Up in the sky appeared many versions of the earth forming a spiral loop above the activation ceremony. Mother Earths, from many levels of the multiple-dimension, had projected their astral forms to these events, bathing in the positive love vibrations that were being shared. They would take this healing energy back to their plain of existence to help bring all existence closer to source.

The energy being generated at this event would reverberate everywhere instantly yet some species choose to be as close as they could get. If someone did not fit into this new loving vibration, they had the chance to ride one of these alternate Earths back to their plane. Some of the inhabitants of these alternative reality worlds have the chance to join in the prime third dimensional world created and are no longer bound to it. One could feel their presence on the alternate earth realities and choose one of these realities for their own or help their counter-parts move to a higher understanding of themselves.

As the ceremony ended one could feel our Mother Earth resonate this new nurturing resonance.

Skywise was the first to speak; "we are all made out of star particles just like our sun who has also nurtured our evolution. This is a time to give back some of that life giving energy that has been so freely shared throughout time".

"Even with all you are learning as a species, along with what has occurred in the past few days, it is also very humbling experience to realize just how much we did not know. In many ways our paths to learning is just opening up to us and there is a long journey ahead for all of us".

Like most of the previous events along the tour, the activation left the crowd with new energy. They can now pull from the earth with new energy to give back to Mother Earth as well. Mankind no longer took their energy from each other, unless it was freely given and freely received.

This energy also affected the animal kingdom that had never lost their connection with the earth. They now had a connection with man that was on equal terms. The concept of ownership was part of the primitive past paradigms. Mankind was fulfilling their role as stewards of the planet Earth.

Meanwhile in Peru: The next location with miraculous events was in Peru with BILL and MYRA's team hosting the event. The indigenous Mayan people anticipated these events going on long ago. These prophecies were passed on only through spoken stories among the Mayan elders, which the Mayans rarely shared.

Don Carlos a Great Mayan Shaman; "the Mayan legends foretold, these mice holds great importance in bringing about our dimension shift. The Gateway was described exactly in the tale of this time. We are also aware that it is not only the Gateway causing this giant leap for mankind, but also it is the day before the event when everyone tapped into their heart centers, that was the actual catalyst that ushered in this new age".

"In many ways in recent years, Peru has been a model for the rest of the world when it came to co-existence. Each plant is grown with love energy. You would taste this in our fruit. Our Peruvians have, not long ago, eliminated hunger with a conscious give and take that comes natural to us, as it is only common sense. Gratefulness is shown with the consuming of any of life's gifts and we always gave back to balance what we used. The towns and villages are all gardens shared by the whole community".

"The idea of man being the steward of the land is not a new idea, yet here in Peru, we have mastered the art of stewardship. We have created a perfect mixture of nature, technology, energy use and individual self-governing. A government structure of any kind no longer exists here in Peru as the illusion of safety or protection was ignored by the Peruvians, since we have overcome any fears that made that necessary".

"In the year 2025, Peru eliminated the monetary system along with the government and organized religion. The Peruvians did not outlaw these things, these institutions just lost their purpose, then faded into history. Children are taught to develop their passions along with encouraging their thirst for learning more. This approach to education has a dramatic affect in bringing out the power of self-determination which in turn makes the need for government entities obsolete. You only need a government for those that could not govern themselves".

"At first Peru received a lot of criticism from the rest of the world. Then we quickly began to prosper, becoming the happiest place on the globe. More countries began to see the wisdom in the co-existence philosophy. This wave of enlightenment, which we helped generate, is being continually evolved throughout the world. Peru will always remain the beacon that lit the way".

"Peru is also the leader in creating everything with its own power source, eliminating the need for grid systems that made people rely on others for amenities, like electricity. Lights, cooking appliances, vacuum systems, robots and all other comfort commodities have their own power source. Anti-gravity vehicles with fusion engines replaced all automobiles by the year 2023. Former roadways have become garden pathways".

"We are now taking another leap together with the rest of our Earth family".

"The love vibration here is strong as it is a place loved by ascended beings for centuries. The attendance at this activation now include the masters throughout time from every culture around the globe: saints, sorcerers, shamans, prophets, holy men, scribes, monks, philosophers, seers, scientist, dreamers, watchers, writers, musicians, architects, comedians, gardeners and many other spirits. All have touched creator source in some way throughout all existence. Many have already reincarnated into a physical vessel living in this time stream who remembered who they were. Many others have taken on a third density form to experience the additional five senses that this density has to offer. Still others choose to participate in spirit form yet you will see them as orbs if you are opened to see them".

> **Each sovereign living in Peru brought a mouse from wherever they could find them to the activation. The entire population was sovereign so millions of mice were brought there. This was a tribute to the inspiring role that one brave group of mice, THE TRIBE, had played in the lifting up of our home planet to bring us all closer to Source.**

Wisdom who was the stowaway on this team of mice; "it resonates for me so much that I am choosing to stay behind in Peru to help develop our species here. I have visions of a wonderful society living freely for everyone. Now I have the knowledge for those visions so they can become reality".

> **This activation event is a journey of creation. Elements have come together to form something that has never existed before or has existed just out of range of our self-imposed limits. The sky is the artists' pallets; the air is the musicians' instruments; the wind whispers the most loving profound poetry; light is the inspiration within, providing clarity to detail. Collisions of different intensities form a whisper colliding with someone's ear or a sun going nova all creating something new. Creation is always just beginning and ending. This moment is not the same as the moment that just past. It can never return yet will always be part of existence, therefore, making each moment of time unique to existence. Each moment is made up of the previous moment, so it never really goes away. It just becomes part of the next moment.**

> All thoughts, visions, dreams, realizations and really everything conceived is creation revealing itself. By tuning into creation, we become co-creators because our intent is what brings benefit or harm to others.

Bill gives a summary of his experience; "Creation has no real beginning or end except from moment to moment. The thought of going back to the beginning of creation can never be realized because time is an illusion in the here and now. The present is made up of the past, accumulations of everything that has happened and the future is cause and effect from present occurrences. Many futures exist, we can shape it to better suit our present needs. All of what we conceive of as time exist in the now".

"Almost everyone marvels at the complexities of creation obtaining different comprehensions on an individual basis. What occurred at this activation is a simple attempt to summarize what really took place on this tour".

> This was not the last location for the whole group of exhausted team members, who are now reaching a point where the simple life of desired rest and relaxation, would be the most welcome gift anyone of them could receive. They needed time to assimilate what they had experienced, as the repeated exposure to the Gateway activations had been energizing to each of them and so much had been absorbed.

The islands of Hawaii was preparing for all the teams' arrival. The Hawaiian people had been watching the tour broadcast from the beginning. A special event was planned that would complement and encompass the whole world tour creating a Grand Finale no one would forget.

The celebration of a new era!

CHAPTER 16

ABUNDANCE OF LOVE

The teams arrived at different times with BILL and MYRA's team the last to arrive. Most everyone around the globe would participate in the final event knowing that the energy would reach them even though they were not anywhere near the Hawaiian activation.

The Gateway activation was scheduled for 11:45 pm ending a 48 hour day for the travelers. Traveling through the time zones gave them the extra time for this tour to take place so successfully. This was a record for the history books in many ways.

With just moments to spare, the three teams met on stage at the event. The teams' love could be felt by the whole crowd as these resolute travelers embraced each other, as if they had been away from each other for ages.

Charles shouted out; "**PENNY, BRANDON,** I have so much to tell you".

> The excitement was infectious, rippling outward to all observers. When they all gathered for a group embrace, you could see surrounding them an energy orb of illumination as bright as a miniature star. They had so much to share with each other. It would have to wait just a little longer.

Albert stepped forward; "my fellow galactic family, we have come full circle in many ways. We see the beginning each time we reach the end. We have been gifted with the greatest of all gifts. The harmony of existence has never received our unique contribution before, so we have risen to new levels as co-creators".

"You see my love for my immediate family and friends while you should also see the love I have for each of you".

On the platform, the whole team holding hands encircled around the Gateway facing outward. The mice held on to the humans at each end of their joined hands. The Teams stretched their arms out to the world sharing energy freely, then envisioned a cosmic embrace that could be felt by everyone around the planet.

> **CHARLES, PENNY and BRANDON lifted SCOUT and the other mice up to start the Gateway spinning. The tone coming from the Gateway had changed; the universe that was displayed before was brighter than ever. New energy had been created and dispersed, like a rejuvenation of cells, everything was healthier.**

Visions of a faraway planet appeared in almost everyone's mind. This planet was in a global war with rival nations. Destruction was all around this planet. Many wondered why they were being shown this violent scene at this time of love.

> Tears ran down most cheeks as what looked like the final blows between the nations was struck. The planet was in ruins with almost no one left, then a cry for help was heard by our whole planet, as everyone sent out their love to rescue

the conscious entities that were caught up in this senseless destruction.

The visions continued with us taking these heroic conscious spirits to another planet with life just beginning, giving this struggling spirit group a chance to start over. Our role as consciousness gardeners was now made clear to us, as we relocated the entire group consciousness to fertile ground. We added our special nutrients of love and would continue nurturing this new creation.

It takes awakening real love to ignite the flame of compassion for others to reveal their true life's purpose, as individuals and as a cosmic collective consciousness. The remembering of the path, we almost took in destroying ourselves, was also very revealing, as a wave of gratefulness was experienced by all the observers, as we managed to save another mankind from its own destruction.

The collective thoughts of the audiences was to plan to help this new race of beings forget the terrible destruction they had just left, feeding them with pure love and taking care of all their needs. We planned to create a paradise for them protecting them in every way. We loved them so dearly! This is not good as it is repeating the same mistakes that were made with our own evolution.

Part of our group consciousness saw that these spirits would not progress and would never reach their full potential if we kept on catering to them. These survivors needed to have their own free will and the knowledge of balance needed to be restored. The all-ness of duality has to be realized to make the leap to self-determination. The path of love is a free will decision.

Others within the group consciousness felt that these loved beings would not accept these gifts because they loved us in return for all we had done. Mass agreement was reached as some from Earth acted as soul ambassadors offering the starter gift that was so needed (free will along with the knowledge of duality). This gift would allow them to begin their path to source all over again. The new species accepted the gifts despite what many had thought and the group consciousness had a momentary inner struggle until their balance returned. This struggle appeared in the sky above New Eden as a battle between great cosmic forces creating fables with only half-truth in them.

A small group of humans agreed to enter physical vessels on this new planet knowing they would have to remain there until this race had evolved to where they would become a part of the universe's collective consciousness. This meant thousands of years and many more reincarnations; so they were giving up a lot to help this race we all helped to co-create.

This group that stayed behind had to act against their loving nature to remind this species of the evil we had helped them forget. Both sides of existence had to be shown to them so the new inhabitants were free now to choose their own paths. This was their genesis which they passed from one generation to the next.

A feeling of accomplishment brought happiness to mankind because creating is the most pleasurable thing known at this time. This happiness fueled the love we felt inside. We were now giving back to the universe on a cosmic, divine scale.

We watched as this new civilization took root and the new inhabitants soared; creating on their own.

This all took place within the ten minute activation, as the Gateway slowed to a stop. With the doorway open you could return to this new creation any time you liked. The thrill of co-creation would spark many to wonder were there ways to help other things evolve in the future? We would become their prophets, angels and saints guiding them towards source.

The whole world felt a new sense of response-ability within themselves for this progressive path. Now what must be considered of our planet children? The civilization of this New Eden would not be visited again as a collective consciousness. This spark at the new beginning almost got lost to the field of their individuality.

Many of us would visit New Eden as our own unique collective consciousness, bringingback reports on how evolution was progressing there.

This was truly a Grand Finale that would remain in everyone's heart center for all time. The festivities for the day slowly came to an end as it came time for all the bodies to rest; a new day was upon us.

As the new day approached, people started to wake up and were experiencing new abilities. Most of these new abilities were already within the individuals only now they were enhanced to greater levels. The world awoke to a world of super humans that would have to adjust by collaborating together. The new concept of our organic universe had become common knowledge.

What was once considered extra-ordinary was now common place. What generations had ridiculed as dreams of impossibilities, could no longer be denied. The change was happening.

The greatest enlightenment was the realization that this was just the beginning of a new path. Millions, if not billions and billions of possibilities, lay ahead. We are here to help guide these infinite possibilities. Ego was now a comic relief, instead of a guiding force. It is funny that we once thought *we were the center of the universe*, without realizing so was everything else. Everything has a center.

People woke up to their bodies rejuvenated to a healthy, younger looking version of themselves. The DNA that causes aging was healed. People were no longer carbon-based species, which was discovered after testing; everyone was more crystalline-based, even though our outer appearance did not change much. What was considered junk DNA was now actively providing the body nutrients that it needed to bring about full health.

> Not everything was rosy and clear as there were still those that brought intentional harm. Just by not giving the negative intentions any of your energy, most negative energy dissipates into nothingness.

> Our team of seekers has many adventures ahead of them and some of those adventures may be told at a later time, for now each of us is in their own adventures in this playground of life.

Albert gave his farewell to the world net; "I'm going to continue doing what I love best, contributing value to the growth of humanity. It is such a joy to have you, **SCOUT** and your **TRIBE** now part of our team of seekers".

> The Gateway was given to ZEB, who released the collective consciousness of an entire galaxy, leaving the quasar-shaped vessel, a shell with no essence. Albert placed the continuously, spinning shell in the courtyard of the USE building.

Zeb offers a little background on the Gateway; "**ALBERT,** that Andromeda (the collective consciousness) gave freely to make the Gateway work; she was more like a group of kindred spirit or soul group that would share by voluntarily entering an object as a vessel to stimulate evolution. She was known not only as Andromeda to me, but also admitted to having an alias called Anthony Hoggins, the author of *From Chaos To Order.* That book had celestial origins and was cast aside by almost everyone. Andromeda's essence was what called out to you, **MARY,** when you first discovered the book in the library. The Gateway was no longer needed for humans and many other animals on our home planet to access the multi-density existence to which we belong".

ALBERT; "what is connection to *Andromeda*"? *"That will be another story"!*

In many ways, ALBERT's team was now part of ZEB's crew of cosmic players helping everything move closer to the love source.

Our world made some tremendous leaps and bounds before this story took place. We are capable of so much more. All we have to do is envision what we want, then do it ourselves. Live your visions because they already exist. Dreams and visions are the cosmic conception of reality. You will attract those with similar dreams and together you will build a better existence for all to reap the benefits.

Mankind is making it all up as they proceed. Anything can become real, as more and more agree to its existence. There is more to existence than we can imagine. So the future discoveries are endless.

One individual may see something, then it takes agreement from others to give it more validity. A sovereign does not need validation from others, so they see things that boggle normal perception.

We are all capable of flight as a winged creature. We are just not ready for it yet. Thinking with your heart center will start you on your journey that can lead to many things. We have to take the first step by realizing that what we do have now is not working for the greater good, especially since we are making it all up. Let's make up something that will serve everyone!

Change your paradigm! Change your reality.

THE END

CHAPTER 17

EPILOG

Albert's Journal of the Universe
1st entry
Gateway Origins

September 1st-2025

It has been almost two months since the global tour of the Gateway. Our research continues with many questions still unanswered. The origin of the Gateway is vague. The information we have is full of partial knowledge that lead to more questions.

My ability to observe the multi time streams is stronger than ever as I have traveled to many eras along the prime stream as well as alternate time streams. Our team or family of co-explorers is with me on most of the vision journeys. We have met yet another member that joined the team just recently who calls himself Seth. His birth name does not matter to him or any of us although he says he is from the family Beck. We have also come to know many of the others individual spirit guides or guardian angels other than Zeb.

Seth is a shape shifter whose animal totems are python, eagle, hummingbird, dolphin, wolf and jaguar. His personification of eagle has made him a close friend of Bill. As eagle, Seth is able to see the large landscape of the big picture while also being able to spot the smallest details within that landscape. Bill, with his heightened awareness of observation is drawn to Seth when he is in eagle form. Bill also relates to hummingbird because as hummingbird Seth is concerned with each flower as he comes across it but stores the energy from the flower for his flight into the world. As hummingbird, Seth can make large journeys with detachment from his next energy serving flower. He stores plenty of energy to make his journeys. When reaching the next flower he gratefully partakes in the life sustaining energy. He gives back to mother Earth by spreading the pollen from one flower to the next.

Runner's new friend Purr-puss has warmed up to Seth in his jaguar personification but as python he scares Purr-puss. The mice tribe is also fearful of python; however they are much better at dealing with their fears than Purr-puss.

The people of the world have rapidly adjusted to all the latent abilities that were enhanced during the Gateway tour. This sure is a different reality that it was just a couple months ago.

Myra has tapped the fountain of biological immortality that for so long been out of our reaches. This will bring lasting change to this garden universe. The answers were in man's connection with source that had been severely distorted along the progressive history man has gone through. Technology had to be balanced with spirit along with a paradigm wave that brought down the limitations that man had self-imposed.

The animal kingdom that is developing has been a new awakening for man as we soon realized just how gifted our fellow inhabitants had become along their evolutionary path. Shape shifters like Seth have known all along the wisdom of the animal kingdom. As wolf he can hear on many frequencies that are normally out of our senses. As Jaguar he can smell and track flagrancies from miles away.

There are some shape shifters that change into in-adamant objects such as chairs or tables or rocks. Some change into plants and trees. Just about anything we can imagine has been assimilated by shape shifters. It is amazing the understanding one receives when they become something other than what they think they are.

I have started this journal today because of what happened on our vision journey earlier. The whole team was present as we journeyed once again to the ancient city of Lemuria. We were seeking answers to our questions about the origins of the Gateway, the Andromeda soul group that contributed the essence for the Gateway and how Anthony Hoggins came into the picture. This was the intent that we all projected as our journey began. Where our intent took us was as surprising as our first Gateway activation.

Zeb met up with us as soon as the visions started. Immediately we were in Lemuria approaching a small child with a large bright luminescent field. The child had an innocence that radiated pure love.

As we approached Zeb gave us some background knowledge as to who this child was; this is the first vessel that the Andromeda soul group chose to inhabit to realize this density of existence. Everything is new and wonderful in this playground for these ancient explorers. They have long ago realized their connection with love source so they experience everything with that same energy. You are familiar with pure unconditional love.

Although the child was operating from the physical plain of vibration he knew we were there. He turned and smiled with this playful grin that welcomed us all.

Charles was so excited by meeting this child that his thoughts almost returned us to the lab where our journey began. Mary was able to bring calm back to Charles. We all shared the same excitement on some level.

"I am" said the child. Come with me.

With these thoughts entering our minds we were instantly transported to the Andromeda galaxy billions of years in the past. Here we could meet the individuals from all over the galaxy that came together to make up the soul group inhabiting the small child. All of their stories were part of our new child acquaintance. From here we could witness their individual path to source.

It became necessary to start being more diligent in my recordings in this journal as the task of keeping a record of all this is part of our families shared passion. Sharing our journeys will have impact bringing everyone closer to source self-recognition. That is part of our journey.

Our group experienced the lives/past lives of all the members of the soul group in one instant. It will take a lot more time than that to share these stories. It will be worth the sharing. As you can see we have many stories to tell. One thing I know for sure is that I will continue to reference the experience of today in all my future Journal entries.

For now it may be helpful to recollect the names of some from this soul group. They had many names but they are best known as the lessons they had to overcome. You could sum up all of their names into a few words. The names are just different versions with the same meaning. So you had variations for ego, sorrow, vanity, sloth, greed, revenge, fear, self-gratification and hatred. Their path to overcome led them to have new names that were opposite these names. As they became closer to source their names changed from ego to humility, from vanity to unity. Sorrow became happiness and so on. They became a balance as the mirror image of what they were merged with who they were.

That is the best way I have for describing the names without boring you with a long, long list. In further entries I may reference the name Ego as they were before they became who they were destined to become.

Today was like the ultimate in shape shifting. We may not have shifted on a molecular level but we became part of that entire young child's life as if we lived it. We experienced billions of years' in one instant.

Next we were back in Lemuria embracing the child as one of the family. We call him; I am. He was very playful with his name saying that we are all "I am". We are all source realizing itself; then he giggled.

Next, this young child took us to a point where they made the conscious choice to merge their essence with the Gateway. We experienced the whole progression through time space instantly feeling each experience as we went. The progression stopped long enough for us to watch the ceremony that Anthony and his wife did that breathed life into the Gateway.

After the ceremony, Anthony's wife carefully placed it in storage where it was forgotten about until recently. We even watched as Scout's tribe of mice developed as they were exposed to the Gateway.

Once again we were back in Lemuria with I am. By now we are old friends.

It has been a great honor sharing my story; **I am exclaimed in an excited tone.** Everything has a story so there are a countless amount of stories to be told. I could tell you a story about a tiny rock traveling through time/space that is continually creating new pages to the story. This magical story is being realized a billion different ways and it all takes place on this rock. In truth my story is just one of the stories that take place on this rock. There are so many rocks out there that have the same diversity and therefore just as many stories. How cool is that? We visited a tiny part of the great "I AM".

Our new friend, "I am" laughed and giggled the whole time he was communicating. He was quite amused with the whole cosmic levity of experiencing existence. His childhood wonder was still a guiding force.

We will probable remember "I am" as the child we met in Lemuria even with our knowledge of his role with the Gateway along with the existence that he shared.

After what seemed like many lifetimes we were all back at the lab. Everyone was ready to tell about their journey. We went one at a time relaying our stories with each of our unique perspectives.

Charles said that "I am" would be the coolest kid in our section of the universe if he wanted to be. Now we are even closer to "I am". We are "I am". How cool! We are the coolest kids in our section of the universe. All of us! Everywhere, every-when!

Scout still astounds me with his revelations. He was spot on. All of us are looking for the same thing; he said. The idea that we are all individual sparks that are just different ways for existence to realize itself is not something we had considered until we met our group here. From what I hear even the GREAT I AM is looking for answers from within. This all-encompassing energy is examining itself from every angle possible and we relay information to this source with free will so that every possible outcome is inevitable. We get our truth from within also. That is our connection to source.

I understand the comic cosmic levity and it is quite funny in a weird sort of way. If the GREAT I AM is looking for realization from within then we should be looking there also. Even the source is looking for the source. This is kind of funny too.

Seth shared his experience of shape shifting into an entire galaxy. He could feel the movement of the stars as if they were the blood that pumped through his veins. He could feel the individual consciousness of countless solar systems struggling for life and thriving with life. He felt like he was dancing in the heavens with billions of other dance partners all around him.

Myra had a similar experience of being the entire Andromeda galaxy but observed a weak energy spot in the closest galaxy to her, being the Milky Way galaxy. She realized that this low vibrational spot was where our solar system is and she saw this section heal itself to become part of the abundant health that the rest of the system shared. Myra believed that the dimming took place as war escalated then became healed and brighter as we passed that threshold of self-destruction in 2012 thru 2015. Myra could feel the empathy from the Andromeda galaxy as they reached out creating the healing soul group to help heal their hurting cosmic dance partner.

My dear Mary picked up on this also. She could hear the cries of millions as bombs were dropped as the war paradigm ruled. She also felt the relief then cheers as man realized the self-imposed noose they had around their necks then removed the noose. Mary went on to say how wonderful she felt being witness to all that is being revealed. I cannot express how it makes me feel to travel the depth of the universe with the one's I am closest to.

She still speaks to me guiding these words as I bring them into being within this journal. Mary has been a pillar of strength for the whole team.

Penny has visions that dwarf the fantasy visions she had previously. She has been creating replicas of many species we have seen on our journeys. With today's journey you can see her excitement to start making her hard sound figures.

This concludes this entry for today. The stories that have been left untold will be shared within further entries. Each story may take volumes to share the experiences of many star beings learning about prime creation. These stories are great fun.

End entry,

Albert, signing off for now.

As a student of life with a curiosity for knowledge and guided by inner knowing, subject to change this author allows his child within to help in creation. The playground we live in still has its bullies, so with a humorous/hopeful outlook he brings us through time and space to where planet Earth is achieving potential that many dream/know we are capable of.

As a child this author could see the imbalance of energy in society making him question life; as if he had a distant memory of living on a planet with much less malicious behavior. This memory is prevalent in the story that is shared. This memory of a better existence is inside everyone and maybe most just need a nudge to bring back that memory. They may say; "Ya! I recall a life where love and balance existed naturally, where strife was replaced with creativity making life a greater experience". Or that memory could be so deep and repressed that nothing sparks a light. Who knows? It is this author's intent to place that reminder out there so we can work towards that better reality.

With a vivid imagination one can see the possibilities presented within the heart/mind of the author. He plays with solutions, theories, poseurs, beliefs, and observations to create inspiration along with self-[de]-termination. He plays with language in a way that may create thoughts about word meanings and sentence structures. At the same time he has to conform to learned patterns to make the story comprehensible and fun.

It is his greatest wish that all have great fun in reading what is shared.

www.ingramcontent.com/pod-product-compliance
Lightning Source LLC
LaVergne TN
LVHW041810060526
838201LV00046B/1194